STARLUCK

STARLUCK

By Donald Wismer

DOUBLEDAY & COMPANY, INC.
Garden City, New York

Library of Congress Cataloging in Publication Data

Wismer, Donald.
    Starluck.

    Summary: After escaping from his execution, Paul
joins a secret revolutionary group which seeks to free
the planet from the tyranny and suppression of the evil
Emperor.
    [1. Science fiction]   I. Title.
PZ7.W78035St   [Fic]
AACR2
ISBN: 0-385-17872-7 Trade
        0-385-17873-5 Prebound
Library of Congress Catalog Card Number 81–43375

FOR KATHERINE WISMER LINDER
WITH LOVE

CHAPTER 1

He was leaving the skool when they came for him.

"Son," the shorter one said, "we must speak to you on a matter of some urgency." Paul looked up. The speaker's companion wore the uniform of the Imperial Guard. Paul was awed.

"Me?"

"Don't worry about a thing. Your parents have been notified," the Guardsman said. He took Paul by the arm.

Paul resisted. The shorter one bent down.

"Listen, Paul, this may sound hard to believe, but you might be able to help the Emperor on a matter of state security."

"State security," Paul said blankly.

"Yes, indeed," the Guardsman said, "a matter of the most delicate security."

Paul noticed that the smaller man was dressed in normal street clothes—a businessman perhaps, or a banker.

Paul glanced back at the skool, as if to find refuge there. But the two men commanded his attention. The Guardsman's uniform in particular . . .

Paul associated that uniform with *authority* in its most compelling and respected form. So his decision, based on nearly twelve years of experience, came easily.

"Okay," he said, "where are we going?"

They brought him to a state vehicle parked along the byway—Paul saw the Imperial emblem on its side, and was impressed at the importance of the two men. They slid into the vehicle. The canopy top rose over them, and they moved noiselessly up into their assigned traffic lane.

Paul looked down.

"I've never been in a car this high before," he said gravely. "How high are we, anyway?"

"Three hundred meters," the taller man said, unsmilingly.

"Three hundred meters!" Paul said. He knew that lanes that high were assigned only to the most important people. He was further impressed.

The smaller man, who was obviously older than the other, cleared his throat.

"Paul," he said gently, "we want you to understand what we're doing."

"Sure," Paul said, gazing spellbound out the window.

"Ryfe here," the man said, "is as you can see a member of the Guard. I myself am a psychosocial adviser to the Emperor."

The taller man turned. "Is this necessary," he asked harshly. Paul looked at him, surprised by his tone of voice.

"I think it is," the older man said sharply. "Everyone has the right to know . . ." He hesitated, then said weakly: "At least in an instance like this."

"There's no point to it," the taller man said, but it was clear from the drop in his voice that he was deferring to the other. Paul was astonished. He had never heard of the Imperial Guard deferring to anybody.

Paul looked at the older man with a new wonder. He met cool, almost amber eyes, and a round, serious face, creased by a seemingly permanent frown of concern, and also of purpose. There was something, in the eyes especially . . .

"Let me put it this way, Paul," the man said. "Do you remember a test that you took about four months ago, that some of you kids call the Fortune Hunter's Test—the Autobeneficent Aptitude Test?"

"Sure," Paul said.

The memory was plain. All his friends said that if you did well on the test, you would become a rich man for sure.

"Well, Paul, you 'passed' the test in a sense. As a matter of fact, you outscored anyone we've ever seen. You did something we thought was statistically impossible. What you did, Paul, is that you achieved a perfect score."

Paul felt a spasm of pleasure. A perfect score on anything was not to be scorned.

But he could see that the man was struggling with his words, trying to make something in them easy to understand.

"What that means, Paul, is that you're lucky," the man said gravely. "Incredibly, unbelievably lucky."

"My friends say that if you pass the test," Paul observed, "you'll get rich."

"Oh, you would get rich all right, no matter what you decided to do." Paul noticed that the vehicle was heading out of the city.

The man was acting strange. He began speaking rapidly, as if hurrying around the main point. The words poured out like rattles out of a box.

"We put questions in that test that were far beyond the competence of any twelve-year-old—in fact, that were so complex that only a research scientist and a couple of computers could solve them, and it would take them a month or so. Multiple choice answers, and any of them would appear as good as any of the others to a boy of your age. To someone of my age, for that matter.

"You might guess one out of five, if you were statistically average," the man said. "Maybe one out of four, if you were lucky. One out of three? Not likely. Out of two perhaps? Never. Every one? Impossible!"

This last exploded from him. Paul was startled. He had done well on that test, but this man did not seem pleased at all.

The man went on.

"You know, Paul, we've thought for years that luck was a psychic force, not just an accident. A human trait, like blue eyes—something in the subgenes, perhaps.

"And we've proven it too, Paul. Some people are a little or even very lucky, just as some are a little clairvoyant or telepathic, or left-handed or knock-kneed or bald-headed. Those with luck reach high in management fields, gather together a lot of money and power, marry the most compatible spouses and lead the most satisfying, happy lives you can possibly imagine. It varies, of course, and it is unpredictable. In some it comes and goes in waves; in others it is constant. But you, my boy, you . . ."

The man paused. Paul looked at him, and suddenly he felt a pang of unease. There was something wrong here, something strangely wrong . . .

"You, my boy, scored perfectly. What are you, then? From all we can see, a being of total luck cannot exist, but here you are. Your family was not well off before you were born, but since then they've suddenly become wealthy, for no logical reason so far as we can determine. You've had the best of everything, and are well-adjusted, happy, and intelligent. In the skool, you're at the top of your class. Everybody likes you. Everything's going just fine for you."

"Up until now," the Guardsman said, his voice hard.

"You know, Paul," the man said, his voice changing suddenly, "that theoretically the luckiest man among the Three Hundred Suns is the Emperor himself. He has never let us test it, but it stands to reason. After all, we are not a closed system by any means, and people of luck not only go places, but they have to retain their luck or their skill to stay there—in the Emperor's case, to survive there. Witness all the rumors we have these days about rebel movements and the like."

The vehicle, Paul saw, was descending over a long series of terraced buildings and gardens. He knew them well—his family had its own summer compound in a place like this, although a long distance from where they were.

Then the buildings ended, and there were dunes, a beach, and then the gentle waters of the inland sea rolled beneath them.

"Eight kilometers is enough," the older man observed to Ryfe. The taller man merely nodded.

"So you can see, Paul, why we have to do this," the older man said gently. Paul could see a vague sort of pain in the man's eyes, a regret perhaps. "Your very existence is a threat to the Emperor. A being of total luck—who knows how far you would get? Maybe even to the Emperor's chair . . . He has not survived this long, Paul, by accident."

Shock hit Paul at that moment, shock like a savage blow to the face. His eyes went wide with disbelief as he looked at the older man.

This could not be. The Emperor would not allow this. My mother and father . . .

Ryfe snapped his wrist back in a gesture that Paul had seen countless times in adventure stories on the video. Just like on the screen, a finger blaster snapped into place. A finger blaster—a terrible hand weapon, whose beam meant instant and horrible death.

The vehicle was slowing, slowing—all Paul could see in either direction were the gently rolling waves, now some six meters below.

"No," Paul said. "No!"

The cold voice said, "Your parents have been told of a tube accident—you were burned beyond recognition with twenty others, no apparent survivors. You see why we have to do this Paul? Don't you? Don't you?" The man shook Paul, grabbed him by both arms and shook him, and Paul looked at him and screamed.

And then he was thrust from the vehicle and was falling. A scream rose from him, to be ended by a mouthful of salt water. He plunged deep into the inland sea, and then his body, reflexively, began to struggle to reach the surface.

He broke through the waves, gasping, the water and light blinding and confusing him.

And then he saw it above him, the hovering angel of death. There, in its gaping doors, stood the two men, their bodies bright in the setting sun. The one stood, holding on to the canopy edge, his business clothes billowing around him in the westerly breeze. The other, erect in his military power, pointed a finger at Paul.

What happened next was always a confusion of light and sound in Paul's memory. The flash and the impact drove him beneath the sea, under the rolling waves that the westerly breeze was piling up, underneath the flaming hell that was erupting above him.

All at once, the water was warmer than its usual tepidity. It grew hot. Paul swam blindly away from the heat; then, when his lungs gave him an imperative message, he was scrambling for the surface. He broke through the edge of the waves, sparkling drops flying from him in every direction. And he saw the vehicle, no longer in the air, burning with a fierce light of its own on the surface of the sea, to challenge with its brightness that of the setting sun.

It was not until long afterward that Paul realized what must have happened: that most rare occurrence of all, a defective blaster charge, which had caused the weapon to explode in the face of the Guardsman. And it was long afterward that he first felt sorrow for the two men, especially the elder. Duty, often misguided and painful, always takes with it at least a small amount of courage.

As for now, Paul was alive. So far, he had been lucky.

CHAPTER 2

The fire began to die. Paul dog-paddled and watched it. For a time he had executed a series of "jumps" in the water, submerging himself and then rocketing as far above the surface as he could go, looking for land. All he had succeeded in doing was to tire himself.

If there were land nearby, it was beyond his narrow and wave-edged horizon. Paul was still numb from the events that had overtaken him. If, two hours before, he had been asked to imagine the wildest and most unlikely thing that could happen, whatever he thought of would have paled before what actually had occurred. So many things that he had taken for granted—his reverence for the Emperor, his belief in the Guard's integrity, the comfort of his life at home—even life itself—had been called into question by the events of the past minutes. He was bruised, shocked, angry. And now, as weariness began to creep over his limbs, he realized that he was tired, very tired. He knew that he could not keep on swimming much longer.

And then the sky lit up.

He had not heard it coming. The flitter swooped down on him from nowhere, and he drew back from it in fear. In the glare of its searchlight he could see no details. And, in the suddenness of the apparition, he thought of something.

If he were rescued . . . But what if he were rescued by the Guard itself? What if, when the homing beam on the state vehicle was broken, there had been set into motion at Guard headquarters a frantic effort to find out why, and to make certain that the Emperor's orders were carried out?

Paul knew then that he was doomed.

The Guard, whatever its faults, was not inefficient, and they looked after their own. Within minutes after the vehicle's disappearance, other vehicles would have gone into the air, and they would all converge on the last known location of the state vehicle. That he was not already dead was something to wonder about, and only the distance of the nearest Guard outpost could explain the delay.

But what did it matter? He had to get away . . . Paul turned and swam frantically away from the flitter, from the wrecked vehicle in the water. The searchlight played over the scene, catching him in its beam and passing beyond, focusing on the wreck and then heading toward him again. He dove beneath the surface.

For a long agonizing hour, it seemed, he swam beneath the surface, though in fact it could not have been more than one or two minutes.

Then the pressure of his lungs forced him into the air. He broke through in a circle of blinding light. He heaved a huge lungful of air, and bent his head to dive again.

"Hey, you!" a voice called. "Where are you going? We're here to help you."

Sure, Paul thought, and dove again. But what was the use? They could blast him underwater, as sure as on the surface.

But wait a minute! There was something strange about all this. In all his life, Paul realized, he had never heard of the Guard employing a flitter. It was always the larger, more powerful state vehicles that they used. Never a passenger vehicle. Never a flitter.

He broke surface again, and peered toward the machine which was settling on the water not more than five meters away.

"Take it easy, fella," the voice called. "Get hold of yourself. We're here to help you."

And they were, Paul realized. Hands reached out over the flitter's side, and voices called to him.

He swam toward them.

The hands grasped his, and he was pulled into the cockpit of the flitter. He turned over, and looked into two anxious faces bent over him. Water poured from his clothes, and sank into the cushions beneath him.

The canopy slid smoothly over them, and the flitter rose into the air. Light poured into the cabin. Paul sat up.

The man at the controls turned. "We saw the explosion in the sky," he said, "but we were thirty kilometers away. Still, we knew there was nothing but open sea there, so we decided to have a look. Are you all right?"

The other man said, "Knock it off, Sam. Can't you see the kid's in shock? Maybe his folks were in that wreck."

"It was a miracle that he was thrown free," the first man said. Paul looked at them wonderingly.

Paul said: "It wasn't my folks." He shook himself to clear the water from his eyes.

"See? He's okay," Sam said. "A tough kid, aren't you, sonny?"

Tom, the other man, said gently: "Are you all right?"

"Yes," Paul said, looking around.

What he saw seemed so incongruous after what he had been through that he began to laugh.

"You're fishermen?" He giggled, and then said again: "Fishermen!"

But the laughter left him suddenly. Certain realities began to sink into his mind.

All flitters had radios, Paul knew, tuned to the police band, to receive weather reports and to transmit, when necessary, breakdown situations and accidents. And this was a classic case. The men were required, by law, to report what they had found to the nearest authority.

The flitter was speeding rapidly over the sea, now dark and featureless with the coming of the night. Far away, over the head of Sam, who was piloting the machine, Paul could see the brightening lights of land, as the flitter sped toward it. And then, as if to confirm Paul's fears, the radio snapped into sudden, startling life.

This is Police Central, it said. *The Imperial Guard re-*

ports a probable accident over the Mare Ilirium, latitude fifty degrees seventeen minutes by nine degrees thirty minutes. Any vehicles in the vicinity are asked to be on the lookout . . .

CHAPTER 3

The men looked at each other. "The Guard?" Sam said. "What do they care about a vehicle accident?" Frowns crossed their faces, and they twisted, looking speculatively at Paul.

In an agony of fear, Paul knew that he had to say something, something that sounded right.

"I, uh," he stammered, "uh, my . . . uncle . . . was a Guardsman. He was in the vehicle." He looked at them desperately, his words sounding lame in his ears.

Tom turned to Sam. "Well, that explains it," he said. "You'd better report it. By the way, kid, what's your name?"

Sam cut him off. "I told you before, Tom, that my

transmitter is out of commission. We'll have to wait until we land at my house to report this."

Out of commission!

The flitter sped onward. The lights on the shore seemed to leap at them, and then spread out below in a scattered panorama of luxury homes and resorts. It was no longer than a minute before the flitter began to spiral down, toward a lavish compound of trees and buildings.

The compound reeked of upper class luxury. Paul looked down curiously at an array of swimming pools, game areas, parks, gardens, all nearly buried beneath the flowers and shrubs of fifty different worlds.

A very rich man, this one, Paul thought. Then another thought occurred to him. Rich . . . Then this man must be, in essence, like himself. Very lucky.

Paul did not feel lucky at the moment. For when the flitter landed, then what? What would he do when Sam went to call the Guard? What indeed would he do when the first Guardsman came for him?

Paul gazed unseeing at the bright panorama below him, desperate thoughts filling his consciousness.

Then his eyes took in something so extraordinary that his brain snapped to attention, and he gasped.

He saw a small oblong building in one corner of the compound, a building no different from any of the others, except for one thing. On the building there was an antenna. Or more accurately, a series of antennas, a sort of elliptical compound dish of wires and projections, a tangled mass of convoluted electrical parts. Yet there was no mistaking the styling of it, nor its gleaming newness, nor its extravagant cost.

Paul knew that he was seeing, for the first time, an Empty.

An Empty, or rather "M T"—Matter Transmitter. Even in this day of interstellar technology, an almost never seen mechanism still in its natal, experimental stages. Paul had seen reports of them on the video—how only six were installed even here, on Elsinore, the capital planet of the Three Hundred Suns. How, by using the atomic and gravitational properties of a compound whose synthesis was inconceivably intricate and expensive, an object, even a man, could be reduced in size to that of a neutron, and then translated into impulses and beamed to another Empty where the complex signal was converted again to normal size.

How the Empty, so far, would only work on a line-of-sight basis—that is, as far as the visible horizon. And how, so intensely, the Emperor coveted the Empty, because it would lend itself to the most devastating military uses.

Paul didn't understand the military uses, but he did understand that the machine he was looking at was capable of sending a man from one point to another thirty-two kilometers apart, instantly, with no ill effects of any kind.

Sam, the pilot, saw his fascinated gaze and chuckled.

"That's what it is, all right, kid. An Empty. I'm one of the lucky ones, or should I say, one of the ones rich enough to get a license to set one up. This one is connected directly with Empty Central at Spaceport. It's only twenty-four kilometers from here."

The Empty could not be used for interstellar travel, or so the stories said, simply because its mode of transmission was electromagnetic, and thus limited to the speed of light. No one would ride an Empty beam, which would take two years to reach the star nearest Elsinore, when an interspace starship could make the jump in less than a second.

Still, the Empty held fascinating potential for travel within a planetary system. There was even talk of setting up permanent Empty "jumpers" in deep space, which would hop back and forth through interspace carrying message units for rebroadcast to the opposite side.

But there were already satellite "jumpers," which carried communications among the star systems. They traveled in a permanent "circle" among various jump-points, passing to planet after planet until they needed reservicing. They could not, of course, handle cargo—that was the province of the starships. An Empty jumper could, in theory. But the Empty mechanism was so bulky and so inutterably expensive, that a jumper was not yet practical.

The extraordinary sight took Paul's mind away from his situation for only a moment. The Empty disappeared behind some buildings as the flitter slid gently to the ground. Sam reached up and threw the canopy back, and Paul found himself in the rectangular courtyard of a tall white building, featureless save for a single doorway.

A servant, dressed in lily-white livery, came running.

"George, see to that blasted transmitter in the flitter," Sam said. He turned to Paul. "Come along, son," he said.

"We may as well call the Guard right now. I am curious to find out what this is all about."

Paul's scalp prickled. The last man to call him "son" had tried to kill him. And the last thing he wanted was to talk to the Guard.

The open doorway beckoned. He turned and ran.

CHAPTER 4

The shouts behind him quickly faded and died away. Paul ran purposefully through a maze of white corridors and gleaming rooms. He saw no one. His mind was now working clearly, and he knew precisely what he wanted, and what he had to do. The only question was, could he

He could not return to his family. Painful as it was, he knew that his family would suffer, if they knew he what could he accomplish by his return but to draw his wrath in their direction—

He had to disappear somehow. He had no

idea how—but he knew that he had to do it. He also knew that he had to leave this compound before the Guard came. Already, perhaps, the man Sam and his people had started to look for him.

Paul burst into a room at the end of the corridor where, finally, the whiteness was broken by a series of pastel carpets and wooden furniture, giving the room the impression of a lounge or game room. Across the room was a wide glass window, revealing a garden overlooking the compound. And a door.

Paul was halfway across the room before he discovered that he was not alone.

The woman had been sitting in a chair near the window. Now she was half upright, looking at him with astonished eyes.

"Who are you?" she demanded loudly. Paul saw that, despite his obvious youth, she was a little afraid.

He hesitated, his eyes darting around the room. No, there was no other exit. He must get past this woman.

He ran up to her, and looked into a kindly, fearful young face.

"I'm Tom's brother," he said desperately. "The flitter pile—it's going to overload. I've got to find the mechanic George."

"Why, I thought he was in the landing courtyard," the woman said.

"He's not. Where's his room," Paul said. M confident, he let some authority creep into his voice.

The woman pointed. "Out there," she said. "B a minute. I didn't know Tom had a brother."

"Don't you understand," Paul yelled. "It's a load! The whole place will blow up any r drove straight toward her, and almost pushed her over as he ran toward the door. She moved aside with a jerk.

It was only when he reached the garden that he dared to look back. She was standing there, looking out at him, a perplexed frown on her face. He ran to the edge of the garden and turned a corner.

He never saw her again.

The compound opened up around him. He saw a tangle of buildings. One was obviously a garage for ground vehicles. Another was the power plant, where solar energy fed electricity to the compound. Another, a gymnasium. All in stark, gleaming white. All festooned and surrounded with the foliage of fifty planets.

Many buildings he could not place. But he had eyes for only one thing, and he found it in the far corner, rearing above the other buildings in a tangle of wire and steel. In a far corner, but nearer than he had dared hope.

The Matter Transmitter. His only hope of escape.

Paul knew that his discovery would be almost immediate if he attempted to escape the compound by normal routes. The whole area was too open, too much a luxury spot. Besides, these compounds were known for their security—they went to great pains to guard against thieves and assassins. His only hope was to reach an area where he could lose himself in a crowd, where looking for him would be like looking for a needle in a haystack, or a particular grain of sand on a beach. And, since he could not pilot a flitter even if he could find one, his only hope was the Empty. The Matter Transmitter.

He sped across the compound, running toward a strange machine whose like he had only seen on the video, and without much detail at that. As he ran toward it, its size seemed to grow, until the building which had seemed so insignificant from the air, changed in proportions until it towered over him, overbalanced by the awesome antenna on its roof.

He ran, searching for an opening in the building, scanning its gleaming, featureless white facade.

A shout rang out behind him. He looked back, and saw, beyond the garden, two figures peering over the roof of the building he had just vacated. He saw them gesture at him, and then, with an abrupt movement, disappear.

He turned his face toward the building in front of him, and ran faster. He knew now that his luck would have to be extraordinary to escape. Even if they themselves did not reach him, all they would have to do would be to phone the Empty technician who would surely be inside, with the transmitter itself. Then he would be caught, and delivered to the Guard.

And then killed.

Paul ran.

All at once he saw the door, a black slit in the building. He was through it before he realized that he had reached it. He slid to a stop in a room that opened before him. He thought of it as a room, but it was more of a cavern. Large and high, the room rose around him like the inside of a hollow mountain.

And then with a shock he saw it, rearing huge and menacing in the center of the cavern. An intricate machine with a featureless gray doorway on its face, a doorway that hummed in an unearthly shimmer of sound. The machine itself glowed with the light of a thousand banks and dials, spiraled by metal walkways and alien controls. But it was the doorway that caught the eye, a bare patch of nothingness that seemed to emanate a cold and impersonal blankness.

Empty, it was, in both uses of the term. Starkly, staringly, repellingly . . . empty.

Paul paused before the repellent strangeness of the machine. He tasted fear in his mouth, and for a moment he was still a child, waiting for someone to tell him what to do.

His mind paused, but his body did not. It plunged into the solid grayness of the doorway, melted like wax into the blankness, into the empty Empty screen.

And he was gone.

CHAPTER 5

There was an instant of painlessness, of forgetfulness. His body vanished, replaced by a kind of ecstasy of space and warmth and void. For a moment, it seemed to Paul that nothing but himself existed. That he was empty and full, alive and dead, awake and asleep, conscious and not conscious. As if all paradoxes came together into one whole. As if he himself was one, and whole.

Then he emerged into a place of blinding light and heat. He fell upward and outward, into disorientation and confusion. His ecstasy disappeared as if it had never been. His body flung outward, and sprawled in a tangle of arms and legs on a floor of polished vinyl. His eyes were suddenly inches from the self-cleaning whiteness, its spotless brilliance dazzling and disorienting him.

He had traveled through the Empty, he knew. He had done something that only a few people had done before. He had been a part of an electromagnetic beam, if the news reports could be believed. He had *been* an electromagnetic beam—or so he thought. And now . . .

Paul raised his head with a jerk and looked around. He saw a roped-off area in front of him, and a dozen gaping people standing behind it, looking at him. His head swiveled, and he saw behind him the awful swirling grayness that he had seen once before—the terminus of the Empty.

He bounded up and turned toward the roped-off area. He now knew where he was, and he knew what he would do.

The people there, behind the rope—they were tourists, come to see a real Empty. And behind them, there must be a door. And behind the door, the entrance to Spaceport. And in Spaceport, the doorways to a hundred worlds. For in Spaceport were the starships.

Again he ran. He dove into the gaggle of people behind the rope, disappearing into a tangle of legs.

It seemed as if his whole life, as far back as he could think, was running, and shouts, and fear.

The crowd gave way before him, and he saw the entrance, where the admission box kept guard and where a line of people stood, hoping to see the Empty. He ran with churning legs, past the crowd and past the box office, and out into open air and a night broken by a thousand lights and a tumult of flitters and sound and people.

He paused, as his mind took in the panorama that his eyes revealed.

He stood on the crest of a hill. Below him, and as far as he could see, was the staggering spectacle that was Spaceport, the incredible kilometers of ramps and flitters and towering, shining starships, their gleaming ebony noses thrust upward into the sky toward the stars that the brightness of the lights blocked out. A hundred starships, a thousand starships—the wanderers from three hundred worlds, laden with rare instruments and spices, with strange foods and herbs, with colors and scents, touches and tastes and sounds. They stood proud and tall, the cells of the lifeblood of an Empire, its cornucopia of necessities and of luxuries, of basics and of wealth beyond imagination.

They stood with the promise of refuge, Paul thought. They stood clearly as instruments to take him away from Elsinore, away from the Emperor and from the Guard that was on his trail. He did not know how he could do it, but he knew he must.

He would climb aboard one of those ships. He would let deep space be his hiding place.

But as for now . . .

Paul looked frantically around. He was on a long street full of people, a street that disappeared in either direction, filled with glaring lights and bright facades.

It was like an amusement park, only more sophisticated. Bars, night spots, eateries, all vied with one another for the legions who thronged around them. It was a giant tourist trap, a place for the new arrivals from the outer worlds of the Three Hundred Suns to relax from the two-day journey and the inevitable delays at customs.

It was a place of strange costumes, of odd-spoken people, their peculiar ways of walking conditioned by other gravities, their incomprehensible mannerisms the product of divergent and, in some ways, fantastic cultures.

Paul had been there before, but only during the day when activity was at a low ebb, and then only with his family on a trip to the city. He had never seen it pulsing with its full nocturnal life as it was now, somehow repellent in its glitter and superficiality.

But the crowd was a lifesend. He plunged into it and found an immediate anonymity. He became the merest unit in a melting pot of strangers who knew not one another, and cared nothing for those moving around them. He was as if in another world, a world of pleasure-seekers who ignored one another, and yet found a dull satisfaction in the crowd, and in the secondhand, tasteless joys of the nightclubs around them.

As the Empty fell farther and farther behind him, confidence began to return to Paul. He knew there was no way that they could easily look for him among all these people. He knew further that they would not dare to disrupt the vibrant nightlife that provided the capital with so much wealth and influence. While the Guard was powerful indeed, nonetheless it took great pains to preserve the Emperor as a picture of tolerantly beneficent rule. The Spaceport merchants were content, but they would not put up with an armed search in the midst of their busiest time of day.

Paul's walk slowed. The logic of the situation proceeded in his mind. He knew that while he might be safe for now, it would not be so by morning, twelve hours away. The nightlife, intense and vigorous though it was, would fade with the coming of day. The merchants would not care if the Guard were about then, because business would be in no way affected.

Therefore, Paul reasoned, the crowd was not enough. He would have to find someplace dark and secret to wait out the day—someplace where no one could turn him in, simply because no one would know he was there.

And furthermore, someplace to sleep.

And he was hungry.

Paul walked slowly, and as he walked, he grew more and more worried. There were no alleyways, since all deliveries came by flitter to the rooftops. Once in a while there was an alcove, but always well lighted, and always nothing more than an exotic entrance to a night spot, brightly lit and well traveled.

He walked two kilometers, and nowhere did he see any possibility of a hiding place.

Little by little, though, the character of the night places changed. They became cheaper, and less pretentious, and their patrons rougher and more violent. It was good, in a way—Paul found an automated restaurant, and relieved his hunger. But when he emerged and started walking again, he discovered that fewer and fewer families were passing by, and that consequently he was becoming more and more out of place.

The fewer people of his own age he saw, the more uneasy he became.

Finally, on the corner of a street surrounded on all sides by tawdry dancing places and bars, he stopped and debated with himself whether to turn around and head back the other way.

And then, nearby, he saw something that drove a new thought into his mind.

He saw a visiphone.

Immediately his mind turned to his family. He thought of the worry that must be touching them, or even worse, the despair at hearing of the "tube accident."

The thought of the "tube accident" made Paul angry. He knew that so far, he had been able to do nothing to strike back at the Guard in any way. Certainly they must have been disconcerted by his escape from their trap, by the series of circumstances that had enabled him to avoid the death that they had planned. But if his family thought that he was dead in an accident, and if the Guard eventually caught up with him, his family would never know the duplicity and evil of the Emperor.

That, at least, he could change.

Paul wavered. On the one hand, he entertained no false hopes that he could go back home. He was young, but he was not an idiot.

On the other hand, he knew that he could reassure his family that he was still alive, and that he could save them the suffering they would feel at thinking him dead.

The child in Paul called to him to go to the visiphone, to see once again the kind faces of his mother and father. But the man in him continued to reason, and the struggle finally reached a resolution.

For Paul knew that, the Emperor being so concerned to find him, his parents' phone would be tapped. With a cold precision, his mind realized that not only would the Guard be able to trace his call, but that he also might put his family in mortal danger—the Emperor, after all, would not want people to brand him as a child killer.

Paul had two choices: he could revenge himself on the Guard, reassure his family, and gain an instant of personal comfort; or he could avoid the slightest possibility that they would be threatened by his own situation.

It was better, Paul decided, that they have a period of grief, than that they expose themselves to the ruler that Paul had now seen revealed in all his duplicity.

"Hey, kid," someone slurred loudly. Paul looked up, into the face of an old man staggering toward him.

"You got any money," the drunken voice said. Paul looked coldly at him.

"No," he said. He looked past him, toward the phone.

Then, painfully, he turned and walked away.

CHAPTER 6

A circus. Paul saw it down a pastel side street just off the main boulevard, in an open place of tents and neon lights. Almost automatically he turned toward it. It seemed to offer a break in the dreary monotony of the area, in the overpowering and stifling *adultness* of the places around him.

As he approached it, he saw at once that it was unlike the nightclubs in one essential aspect: it offered the possibility of concealment. For here was a circus that was trying to capitalize on the new nostalgia that was booming through the Empire for the symbols and images of antiquity.

There was a jumble of wagons and a Big Top, a maze

of booths and rides, of concession stands and cages. There were all the trappings—carnival barkers, freak shows, halls of mirrors, wild rides and games of skill. And there was the overpainting of an interstellar civilization— animals that the ancients had never seen, foods that they could not have imagined, sights and sounds that would have staggered them, if they could have been awakened to see them.

A ramshackle outfit for all that, Paul perceived. Traveling from world to world, trying to arouse interest in old wonders in this, an age of wonders. Poor, probably always on the brink of bankruptcy. Evidently the nostalgia boom was less than a boomlet on Elsinore; even now, at the peak of a good business night, there weren't many customers here—they could find more satisfying happenings in the sophisticated inns along the boulevard.

But Paul cared for none of this. He saw a hundred different hiding places in the packing cases and cages, places where, if he were lucky, he could lie up while the night spent itself, and the day came . . . and went.

The Guard was probably already on his trail, he knew. Beginning at the Empty terminus, the Guardsmen would mingle casually among the patrons of the boulevard, out of uniform, just ordinary people, looking for a lost boy of about twelve, their brother or son or friend. And gradually they would pick up his trail. Gradually they would find people who had seen an unescorted boy wandering down the street, going nowhere in particular. And while it would take them awhile, eventually they would come to the street corner that he had just passed, and then they would turn . . . where?

So Paul tried to make himself as inconspicuous as possible. Rather than walking into the fairway, where the crowd was too sparse for anonymity, he went instead behind the concession stands and game booths. He walked into places where the shadows hid him, and where no one's eyes would remember.

He found himself in a place of darkness and shadow, broken by gaps in the booths and cages where light streamed through, and made the shadows even darker. He paused to let his eyes adjust themselves, while his ears heard the sounds on the fairway, and other unnamed noises closer at hand.

All at once he realized that he was straining his senses, standing tensely and straining to see and hear and smell what was around him. It was the strangeness of a place where people did not normally go, where he did not *belong*.

He was surrounded on two sides by the backs of booths and concession stands. Behind him was the gap through which he had come. In front was an increasing blackness, where the booths created a tunnel of sorts, and where light shot only intermittently through the shadows.

A thud sounded on his left, and he jumped. It came again. His eyes picked out the back of a booth, and then suddenly he knew what it was. It was a game wherein someone threw a ball at a pile of rounded blocks, trying to win a prize.

He sensed other things, too, some of which he did not recognize. There was a low animal smell, a peculiar disturbing scent faint in the air, speaking of a beast or beasts for which he did not have a name. From a darkened booth in front of him, a little to the right, came the purr of some sort of machine, but running no mechanism that he could see. And over it all were the shouts and cries of the people on the outside.

Paul's mind was emptied by the strangeness of it. He stood still for long minutes, listening to the life that came to his ears. He was nervous, undecided.

Then, slowly, as if shaking off an intolerable burden, he took a step, and then another. He moved toward the area of increasing shadows, where the lights came fewer and dimmer, as if they fronted an unused portion of the fairway where no one was.

The animal smell increased. And now there came other sounds, unmistakable motion behind some of the makeshift structures. Startled, his ears picked out a low moan from the right. Then one on the left. Suddenly there was a series of frantic twitterings, and then muffled flappings as of great wings straining to leave the ground.

The twittering ceased. Then for a moment there was silence, with the ghastly undertone of a huge body moving slowly across a wooden floor. The twittering came again.

Packing cases, cages. Here must be the rear of the place where the animals were kept, the animals from three hundred strange worlds among the scattered stars. Paul's neck prickled with the stirrings around him, the upwellings and slow rhythms of alien life.

Somewhere ahead, he knew, there must be the entrance to the Big Top itself, through which these animals were periodically paraded. Or perhaps he was behind showcases, darkened now at the tail end of the business day, where the beasts that could not be trained were put on display for their strangeness and perhaps their ghastliness.

He stopped again, uncertain. He could not shake off an oppressive feeling of danger here, a choking sensation of peril that he felt, surrounded by these . . . things . . . that he could not see.

And then it came, a terrible roar from his left. One of the structures shook violently. The scream wailed and shrieked, on and on with no apparent pause for breath, falling through octaves of inhuman sound, like a beast in the throes of the most terrible, howling rage.

Paul shrank from the sound. He saw the back of a cage shake, and then the ground bounced as some gigantic blow passed through it from the cage. The scream kept growing louder. He began to believe that his eardrums would split away and crash, reeling into his numbed and staggered brain.

Still a shred of reason clung to him. He turned to run past the cage into the deeper shadows.

But he saw something that stopped him cold.

Away down the cavernous path before him, breaking the prevailing darkness, was the bobbing and weaving of some sort of lantern, coming toward him.

Someone, Paul realized, was coming to see what the noise was all about.

He looked frantically around. The other animals were aroused now, and Paul was surrounded by a chaos of bangings and twitterings and cryings and laughings.

But there were packing cases all about, some no more than a meter high, others larger, to one that stood at least four meters high and as many wide.

A shorter case beside the big one indicated definite possibilities. He ran over to it, and found the smaller one hard and full, unpacked as yet.

He tapped the larger one, and the hollow thump was lost in the screeching din around him.

He looked around. The lamp was closer. Behind it he could see the outline of a man.

Paul hoisted himself up onto the smaller crate. The lantern described a bright circle of light as the keeper swept it over the area, seven meters away.

Paul reached for the top of the packing case, and swung one leg over. The bottom of the case could be covered with broken glass or poisonous snakes, for all he knew.

The light swept toward him. With only the slightest hesitation, Paul threw his other leg over the case, and dropped lightly into the darkness below.

He landed softly on what was clearly the bottom of the case, on a scattering of straw or hay. He crouched panting, trying to keep muffled and to himself, despite the din.

The light described an arc over the top of the case.

Paul found a crack in the side of the packing case and looked out. The man with the lantern was peering between packing cases and around the edges of the cages. The din continued.

Finally, the man apparently decided that he himself, as much as anything, must be causing the commotion. Paul saw him look for a last moment, and then turn and walk back toward the Big Top, leaving behind a tumult of catcalls and ravings.

Then slowly, the din subsided. Paul's scent was drowned in the dusty odor of the packing case. The animals sniffed and listened for something unusual, and found nothing.

Finally the heavy animal gave a last scream. The cage jumped once more, and there was silence.

Paul sank down onto the straw of the case, and breathed a long sigh.

In his weariness a thought struck him, and he almost laughed out loud.

Lucky, he thought. If he were truly lucky, he would be with his family. He would have failed the test. In fact, Paul thought insanely, if he had been truly lucky, he would not have been lucky at all.

He realized that there was no point in going on. This packing case in the midst of a hoard of unknown animals, in a circus that he did not know, was as good a place as any.

He was tired of it all. He was dead tired.

CHAPTER 7

Paul awoke with a shock and sprang upright. He looked around frantically.

He found himself in a rectangular box filled with sunlight. Seemingly from the sky, there fell large clumps of hay and straw.

Paul opened his mouth to cry out, and then thought better of it. He moved to the crack in the side of the packing case, and peered out.

Two young men stood there, wielding pitchforks from a pile of straw rakings, throwing the straw up and outward, so that it fell into Paul's refuge. They laughed and hurled hay and epithets at one another as they worked.

Paul looked past them and his jaw sagged. Where the

day before there had been booths and cages, there now was open space and scattered wagons, and a milling confusion of stevedores. The circus was breaking up. It was coming down around him.

Paul stared at the boys. One was tall, with a shock of blond-red hair and an amiable look to him, dressed in the classic stevedore outfit, coveralls and a khaki shirt. The other was shorter and blonder, with a more serious face—and yet, Paul guessed, neither one was much older than himself.

Paul was wondering how they were going to react to the sight of him climbing out of the packing case, when he saw something that almost caused his heart to stop.

There, some ten meters away, standing tall beside a wagon, talking to the mustached driver, was the unmistakable figure of an Imperial Guardsman.

Paul's eyes went beyond the Guardsman and saw another, maybe eighteen meters away, talking to a stevedore. And there on the right another, circulating among the wagons.

Paul sank back against the growing pile of hay.

So they had traced him here.

Now there was no question of offering the two young men anything to think about. Now there was only the question of silence and the cold taste of fear.

Paul watched the Guardsman that was closest to him. He saw the mustached man shaking his head, and for added emphasis, gesticulating with his hands in a universal sign of negation. Paul saw the Guardsman turn away.

And then something happened that was so singular that Paul was to think about it for a long time to come.

As the Guardsman turned his head, the mustached

man turned and seemingly looked straight into Paul's prison, straight into his eyes as they peered forth from the crack in the case. Paul quailed before the intensity of that gaze, the piercing intentness of two coal-black eyes, an impression of power and coldness and strength.

For a moment, Paul believed in the deepest part of his soul that this man *knew,* that he held Paul in the grip of his knowledge and his whim.

Then the man opened his mouth, and called out in a deep bass voice.

"Hola! Shimmy!" he called.

The red-haired boy turned.

"Aye," he shouted.

"Ready for the griff?" the man sang.

"Aye," the boy yelled. The two dropped their pitch-forks and moved back. They were looking toward something on the right, out of Paul's field of vision.

A clank of machinery sounded. The mustached man's bald head turned toward it. The turbulent eyes broke away.

Paul became aware that he was holding his breath. Slowly he let it out, and relief came over him.

So the man had not been looking at him after all.

The clanking sounded nearer. Paul frowned and moved to the side, trying to see as far to the right as possible.

No good.

He looked back, and then snatched his eyes away from the hole. The Guardsman was looking this way now, his eyes focused on something beyond the case.

Paul's suspense did not last long. All at once, something blocked out the sun. Paul looked up, and gasped.

He looked at a rectangular shadow surrounded by sunlight, a huge blot in the sky. Topping it was the protruding girder of an atomic crane.

The object swayed into full view, some three meters above the top of the packing case, swinging gently as the crane moved closer.

So the box was not for straw alone! Paul crouched tensely. The crane maneuvered the object into position, directly above the packing case.

And then Paul found a surprising thing.

After all these hours of fear and running, his fear had begun to go away.

Perhaps it was that he was so used to it now, that it was no longer a factor in his decisions. Perhaps he was numbed. Perhaps, even, after overcoming all the dangers he had faced, he was finding an inner reservoir of self-confidence—even courage.

Swiftly he considered the situation. Obviously he could not permit himself to be crushed by the object that the crane was bringing toward him. The alternative was to reveal himself.

Paul looked through the crack. The Guardsman was still there, his eyes focused on the object above Paul's head.

Still, perhaps even with the Guard there, he could still get away . . .

But wait! Was there another alternative?

Paul's eyes narrowed into slits as he studied the object swaying above him. It was big. Surely it would almost fill the packing case. Surely it would . . . almost.

The straw! What was it there for? Obviously, to cushion whatever was in that thing above him. But then, they must have accounted for the straw when they built the packing case. In other words, the object above him must necessarily be shorter than the packing case.

If that were true for the height of the box—if those outside wanted to cushion it from the bottom—surely they would want to cushion it from the sides as well.

Quickly Paul measured with his eyes. Yes! It did seem a little narrower than the box. Perhaps narrow enough for his body to remain there too.

Tensely, Paul watched the object as it began to descend. It seemed to get larger and larger as it came down, as it blotted out more and more of the sun.

The swaying had almost stopped. Gently, as if handling something fragile and soft, the crane allowed the object to touch the inside top of the packing case.

The swaying stopped altogether. For a moment, there was only silence, as the crane operator made certain that the object was positioned correctly.

Then, the object began to descend. Paul saw that whatever it was, it had a woven metal floor, a strong molybdenum-steel alloy. It was obviously very heavy.

Paul knew that it was probably too late to save himself. Even if he shouted, even if the boys heard him, they probably could not stop the crane before the object had crushed Paul beneath.

Paul's mind worked furiously. There was only one chance. Even with its weight, perhaps he could push it aside just enough so that it would slide down beside him, rather than on top of him. It was dangling from only one hook. Perhaps he could move it.

But he had to wait until just the right moment. If he pushed it too soon, the crane operator would see the movement and try to correct it.

Paul crouched down. The object stopped moving, with only the slightest centimeter-wide sway in the exact center of the box.

A good crane operator, Paul thought.

And then it began to descend again.

Paul waited until it was only a few centimeters above his crouching body, only about a meter from the bottom of the box. If it continued on its present course, there would be room for only half of Paul's body.

Not enough, Paul thought!

He reached up and grasped the side of the object. With his feet braced as well as they could be on the straw-covered floor, his back on the packing case's wooden side, he gently began to push.

For a moment nothing happened, and the object continued on its inexorable downward course. For a moment, Paul tasted fear again.

He pushed harder.

The object grazed the top of his head.

Then, bit by bit, it began to move aside.

When it finally settled to the straw (Paul had to hastily snatch one foot away), there was perhaps three fifths of a meter of breathing space.

He heard an explosion of curses. He looked out the crack.

The curses were coming from the crane operator, out of Paul's field of vision. The mustached man on the wagon had his head cocked toward him, listening gravely.

"I thought I had it just right," the voice said. "It fell out of position at the last minute."

"Close enough," the mustached man said, and looked back toward the box. Was that a smile on his face?

The two young men seized the pitchforks, and once again straw cascaded onto Paul's head. Paul kept his crouch beside the crack in the side of the case, arching his back to leave a breathing space for himself.

He let the straw cover him.

He heard the boys climb on top of the object in the case and throw straw from it into the gaps around the sides of the box. They tramped it down, while Paul arched his body and resisted.

Then there was silence for a moment, and the cage trembled. Paul heard the sound of nailing.

The top was going on the packing case, Paul thought.

Outside, the Guardsman turned away.

The nailing ceased, and the boys jumped off the top of the packing case. Paul saw them walk up to the mustached man, who gestured them off to another job.

Paul began to relax. He turned away from the crack.

There was no other choice, his mind thought quietly. Wherever I'm going now, it is not to certain death.

Just probable death, he thought, and chuckled to himself.

Just then, his nose caught a strange scent. Suddenly it occurred to him that he did not know the nature of the object in the box with him.

Probably some sort of machinery, he thought. He scraped at the clinging straw around the sides of the object. To his surprise, his hands revealed to his straw-encumbered eyes a woven steel screen, not a solid surface.

He cleared the straw from the screen and tried to peer within. For a moment, a few strands of straw obstructed his vision, and brusquely he brushed them aside. The scent was stronger now.

As his eyes adjusted to the deep shadows within, the object, illuminated as it was solely by the light streaming through the crack in the packing case, Paul's nose crinkled a little. There was something familiar about that scent.

And then his eyes saw it, crouching in the corner of its cage.

Paul thought for a moment that he was looking into hell.

CHAPTER 8

The red eyes burned at him with a frozen expression of feral savagery, of ghastly, unearthly hate and rage. It had a yellow, wrinkled face, which glistened like melting snow, accentuating the searing fire of the wide open, staring eyes. Its yellow, smooth body was vaguely man-like, but built with such plain efficiency of limb and sinew that the effect was more cat than man. Its fingers were rending claws; its toes built for gripping and tearing. The jaw beneath the awful eyes was recessed like a shark's, with row upon row of gleaming, razor teeth. It was only slightly bigger than a full grown man, but radiated a strength and ferocity that transcended anything any man had ever known.

Paul's face was white and sweaty as he stared at it through the bars, stared into the most awesome image of savagery that he had ever seen. He was staggered by it even in the growing courage of his mind, staggered and transfixed by its transcendent wildness. Alien, yes, alien in a way that was the quintessence of alienness, the negation of all things positive, kind, gentle. Here was a polar *something,* a being on the archetypal end of a spectrum of ruthlessness before which Paul's consciousness retreated, sinking unnerved into a morass of superstitions and dread.

It was a long moment before it sank into his dazed brain that the thing was not moving, was not showing any signs of life. Paul began to see that there were shackles about its arms and legs and chest, bolting the beast to a corner of the cage. The thing was chained and unconscious, despite the awful openness of its eyes. It was heavily drugged, Paul finally realized.

As any savage animal would be, Paul thought, for an interstellar journey. Even so, the effect was more uncanny than it would otherwise have been. If this beast seemed so terrible now when it was asleep, what in the name of all reason would it be like awake?

It was a griff. Paul had heard the mustached man pronounce the word, and he had not understood. Now he did. It had to be something from a newly discovered world, a world that had never known humanity before. Otherwise, Paul knew, with the effect this thing would have on any observer, he would have heard tell of it.

The prison rocked, and Paul knew that . . . they . . . were being loaded onto a motorized wagon. He looked out of the crack, and tried to shake himself loose from the idea that he was being watched from behind.

They were rolling now. Paul saw an open, littered field sliding past, and from glimpses behind and in front concluded that he was a part of a procession of wagons, rolling out of the parade grounds.

And then after a while, the vast panorama that was Spaceport opened to Paul's eyes. Only now it was immeasurably nearer—in fact, they were right on the edge of it. The spaceships towered more impressively, and he saw with a deep immediateness its pulsing and complex life.

Here was a group of dignitaries, statespeople from another world. There, a gaggle of students, ohing and ahing at the new and strange sights around them. For a moment, Paul caught a glimpse of a titanic, snake-like tube, slithering forth to suck grain from a monstrous cargo ship. But it was blocked out by an animal so immense that Paul could not believe that a poor circus like this one could own it—until he realized that it was not part of the circus, but of a "cattle" ship, making a run of fresh meat for the gourmet trade of the Emperor's world.

There were checkpoints and customs stations, officialdom in all its regalia, and the ubiquitous presence of the Imperial Guard. Paul watched these narrowly, but they showed no interest in the tattered ranks of a hand-to-mouth circus of no particular distinction.

But their interest was not entirely absent. He first guessed it when his wagon stopped abruptly, throwing him against the hay. And then, from the intermittent starts and almost immediate stops, he knew that each wagon was being checked somewhere up ahead. He hoped that it was the usual customs routine.

After an interminable time, Paul began to distinguish voices. Finally he could make out words.

". . . matter of routine. Nothing against your outfit per se."

Another voice came loudly.

"We have never had a 'heat check,' as you call it, before. You can take the internal temperature of a wagon, to be sure. But what can it possibly reveal?"

Paul recognized the voice.

They moved a bit nearer. Paul thought, oddly, that the mustached man was speaking with much too loud a voice under the circumstances.

"Sir, I assure you that stowaways find no mercy with us. They tend to . . . disappear . . ." The word trailed off into nothing.

". . . for your protection." The Guardsman's voice was low, and Paul could not make out all the words. ". . . accuracy . . . fugitives . . . all possible precautions."

"You must realize that the animals vary in their external temperatures," the voice said loudly. "Every one is different."

"Well, you just tell us the right temperature," the Guardsman said, "and we'll spot anything unusual."

The wagon moved still nearer. Paul, straining to the side of the crack, saw that the procession of wagons made a slight turn up ahead. Just beyond he could make out a Guardsman seated at a portable console, watching tracings on a greenish screen. The bald-headed man, his mustache bristling fiercely, was talking animatedly to one of the three or four armed Guardsmen standing around.

"The wagon contains fourteen sick-sees," he said angrily. "Their mean body temperatures are probably around forty-one degrees Celsius, since they are essentially birds."

"Well, this jury-rig is not all that precise," the Guardsman said, "but we could tell if anything funny was in there. How about it, Kuseck?"

The import of it all suddenly sank home. They were checking each wagon for body warmth. They were looking for him!

The console operator said: "Blast these obsolete units. All I get is a vague blob of heat—I can't count how many there are in there. But he's right, it is around forty-one or so."

"Okay, move it on," the Guardsman said. The procession jerked into motion, and then stopped as the next wagon reached the machine.

Paul stood immobile for a moment, his heart sinking. Then he knew that he was facing another crisis, another threat of imminent capture.

He could not get out of his box. He could scarcely move.

"This one contains no animals," the mustached man said. "Just some machinery."

"He's right," Kuseck said.

The wagon jerked into motion once more.

Then Paul began clawing. He started to burrow a hole in his straw, knowing that he had to risk the noise. He thrust armfuls of the straw behind him, between his legs, almost choking on the dust.

"A coemaranthus—a 'false dragon,'" the mustached man said. "Since it is a reptile, it should not be hotter than the air around it."

"Twenty-eight degrees," the operator said.

"Move on."

Paul reached a corner of the cage, as sweat poured from him. There was barely room to pass. He felt painfully the cold metal on the one side, and the rough wood at his back, as he burrowed around the corner.

"This one has a wier-dog," the mustached man said. "We have caused it to hibernate for the trip."

"Too cold for anything else," Kuseck said.

The wagon jerked again.

Paul thought he was stuck for a moment, and he became frantic. He freed himself, and reached the far corner of the cage.

He could not turn this corner—he himself had seen to that. He calculated that he was about half a meter from the chained body of the beast inside the cage.

It was the best he could do.

"A griff," the voice said loudly.

Paul froze, his sweat streaming into the dry, thirsty straw.

"Usually about forty-three degrees," the man said, "but it is sedated. I would guess about thirty-six, but we have not had this animal long. I am not sure."

There was a silence. Paul held his breath, and closed his eyes to keep out the sweat.

"Damn this old equipment," the operator said finally. "I'm getting almost a double image here."

The other Guardsman's voice showed interest. "How's that?" he said.

"Well . . ." Kuseck said. Paul guessed that he was adjusting the controls. Then he heard the voice say angrily:

"Blast it, now I've lost even that."

"Well, how about the temperature," the other Guardsman asked.

"Thirty-seven," Kuseck said disgustedly.

There was another pause. Paul could almost see the Guardsman's eyes fixed speculatively on the packing case, his mind working with suspicion.

Finally, the voice said: "Still getting a double image, Kuseck?"

"Not now. It's probably this blasted machine more than anything else."

Another pause. Paul resisted the impulse to wipe the sweat from his eyes. Surely motion would register on the machine.

"All right. Move on."

And relief came over Paul again, like a puff of fresh air. He waited until the wagon was on the move again, before dragging the back of his right sleeve across his closed eyes.

Laboriously he burrowed back to the crack in the packing case. Once there, he sank down wearily, disregarding the straw that poked at him.

He looked out. Now they were among the starships, towering monsters pointed boldly at the sky. At one time, Paul would have been overawed by them, fascinated by their sleek lines and their dull blackness which, along with collectors deployed during flight, absorbed power from the sunlight. But now Paul gazed dumbly, his mind dormant, and the ships went past his gaze like a moving picture, devoid of all vitality and interest.

And then even that was blotted out. The wagon entered the wide doors of a cargo hold. Paul saw rows of wagons in a low room as they were jockeyed into position.

He saw the faded colors on the wagons, the insignia of a time gone by.

Then his wagon became part of a row itself, and stopped; Paul saw other wagons slipping past his, to take their places in line. Finally he was facing a second row of wagons end to end, featureless in their sameness.

At last he heard the dull clang of the cargo doors being closed.

And slowly, reason seeped into his brain, and found him there, crouching in the hold of a starship, a lost child in hunger and darkness.

And he was headed for the stars.

CHAPTER 9

He slept. Exhausted in the heat and stifled by the closeness of his cage, he slept in the dried salt of his sweat and the musky scent of the savage beast at his side. Even the bump as the starship left the ground did not awaken him, though it was exceptionally ungentle, a testimony to the ship's worn and aged solar collectors.

A loud rasp brought him startlingly awake. Peering out of the crack, he looked directly into the beam of a flashlamp, which caused him to jerk his head aside, blinking. He heard a rasp again.

It suddenly struck him why. The nails were being pulled from the roof of his prison.

A loud thump sounded on the side of his cage.

"All right, you," a voice said. "You're coming out!" The case thumped again.

"Quiet! You will waken the griff," another voice rumbled. Paul recognized it—it was the mustached man.

Paul's heart sank. So he had been seen! And now, just when he was headed for deep space, hoping to emerge forty-eight hours later and lose himself on a new and unknown planet, he was caught. He tasted the bitter acridness of despair.

But there was also a sense of relief. He was not running anymore.

The rasps ended. Paul heard the sound of footsteps on the top of his prison, and then a silence. The deep voice came to him softly: "Ready, Jonny?"

A third voice answered: "Aye!"

There was a loud groan, and Paul knew that the roof of the cage was coming off.

It ended, and footsteps sounded nearby. Paul looked out. The flashlamp no longer shone directly into his prison, and he could see the tall, red-haired boy holding it, directing it upward. Then the mustached man appeared in his field of vision, and moved until he was facing Paul through the crack in the wooden cage.

"You have a choice," the voice said softly. Paul saw once again the piercing power of the two coal-black eyes. "You may climb out by yourself. Or you may cause yourself some pain."

The words ended, and there was a pause. The baldheaded circusman and his companion waited on the outside, for the cornered fugitive within.

And then there was movement. Grimly, Paul stood up, and reached upward with his hands. He grasped the top of the case, and with a slow movement of cascading straw, he drew himself upward, braced against the side of the griff's cage. Straw fell over the side of the box and onto the floor in front of the two circusmen.

Paul leaned backward, sitting, then pulled himself erect on top of the cage. He stood there, looking down into the eyes of the mustached man, standing in a pool of light on the floor of the hold.

"Come down," the man said.

Paul came down.

The man looked Paul over with a certain cold curiosity, his dark eyes giving no hint of the thoughts flowing behind them. Paul's eyes darted around, seeking some escape. But outside was cold space, and this was their ship.

The man finished his inspection, and then grunted. He turned.

"Come," he said. Pushing Paul before them, the redhead Shimmy and the blond boy Jonny followed.

Now what? Paul thought wearily.

CHAPTER 10

"Who are you?" the mustached man rasped. He stood before Paul in a little room off the main corridor. The two boys waited outside. Once again, Paul was struck by the force behind the glittering black eyes before him.

He drew himself up to his full height and met that awful gaze.

"Who are *you?*" he snapped back. With a great effort of his will, he resisted the almost overpowering urge to look away.

The mustached man smiled. He leaned back and sank into the chair behind him. Then, to Paul's immense re- lief, he slowly and deliberately closed his eyes. Paul felt a momentary, tiny triumph.

"Kid, I will not play a staring game with you," the man said. Paul's triumph vanished. The man went on. "You chose to hide among our cages, and you did it to escape the Guard. Here, we have no love for the Guard. So what we want to know is: why is the Guard chasing a mere boy through the Spaceport slums? In other terms," and his eyes opened to slits, "what does the Guard want of you?"

Paul felt his courage growing. He would concede nothing, give nothing away. He had no more trust for this mustached man than he did in the Emperor himself.

"You didn't," he said coldly, "answer my question. Who are you?"

The man threw up his hands in exasperation. He leaned his head back, and looked at the ceiling.

"Why does this always happen to me?" he inquired of no one in particular. "These kids try my patience." It was only later that Paul would realize the ridiculousness of those words, coming from a man whose patience, among other things, was a legend. Now, however, he only stared back at the man, saying nothing.

"All right," the man said, "but while I am saying this, I want you to think about one thing. I could have turned you over to the Guard on Elsinore. You saw me look into that crack in your crate, and you *know* what I could have done. Think on that, now, while you listen to me; and when I have done you will answer me, you *will* answer me."

He paused to let the words sink in, while Paul's mind worked to find a flaw in the other's logic. Is this a Guardsman's trap, he asked himself frantically. What lies hidden here?

But his mind returned inexorably to the facts. The Guard wanted to kill him, and apparently didn't care when or how. Paul could think of no reason for them to toy with him like this. His mind tried, jumping from point to point in the past hours, and finding nothing to hang onto.

"My name," the man said quietly, "is Ahm Baqa. This is the circus ship *Funakoshi*. We are four hours out from Elsinore, bound for the red planet Shad in the Cygnus region. There we will put on our usual show, and work as long as it profits us. Then we will head for Bora, and from there, Amphor, Cleon, and Potts. We have not yet decided where we will go after that."

Paul's mind had slowed to a near stop. Shad, Bora, Amphor, Cleon, Potts! He'd never been off Elsinore!

"We often suffer harassment from the Imperial Guard. They distrust us for our freedom and our style of life. We are disciplined in the undisciplined and fragmented society on which the Guard preys. But we do nothing overtly illegal; we pay taxes (though not much, since we do not take in much); we make ourselves insignificant and beneath the Guard's attention. They step on us when they notice us; otherwise they leave us alone, and that is the way we prefer it."

Paul's thoughts muttered confusedly in his head.

"We make a living. We enjoy living. Living is the greatest thing we have, the only thing we have, and we do it as well and as fully as we can." He stroked his full, black mustache. "If you stay with us, kid," he said thoughtfully, as if choosing each word, "for any length of time, you will become as hard as Jonny and as kind as Shimmy. You will be strong, stronger than you have ever been before, stronger than you have ever imagined you could be." He paused again, and then said: "You will be able to do anything, *anything,* that you want to do, function easily in any situation, work with any group, achieve any goal."

Suddenly, Ahm Baqa threw up his arms.

"But what is this, anyway," he growled. "The real point is that you need us and we do not need you. Let me put it this way, kid: either you tell me who you are and what you are doing here, or we *will* turn you over to the Guard on Shad like any other stowaway." He regarded Paul grimly, waiting for an answer.

Paul laughed wildly and shouted:

"Go ahead, do it, see what I care! I'll get away again. Nothing can stop me, 'cause I'm lucky! LUCKY!" he screamed, and broke down, hunched over in his chair, sobbing into his knees.

Ahm Baqa watched him, his eyes narrowing. Paul wept from exhaustion and loneliness. Baqa gazed at him, his eyes clouding with thought.

Minutes later he shook himself, and came over to Paul. Gently, he laid his hands on Paul's shoulders, and lifted Paul's tear-streaked face close to his. His eyes looked deep into Paul's, and Paul felt his spasm of despair subsiding before that kind, intense gaze.

Ahm Baqa began to speak softly, never taking his eyes from Paul's face. As the words came, Paul felt his pain ebb away, replaced by emptiness and peace. The time for dissimulation was over.

"I know now, kid," Baqa said, his voice taking on a soothing cadence. "You do not need to tell me anything more. Everyone in the Empire knows about the Fortune

Hunter's Test—we have all taken it ourselves, and some of us know what it truly means."

Paul felt a brief surge of astonishment. How had the man inferred all this from one word he had blurted out only moments ago?

"Let me suggest what has happened to you," Baqa said softly. "You scored high on the test for luck, so high that you exceeded the safety limit that the Emperor's educators have established. You scored so lucky that in a sense you scared the Emperor—he saw your score as a threat. He saw *you* as a threat. So the Guard came after you, and you ran, and somehow you ended up here. Consider this, kid." He paused significantly: "If you are as lucky as you think, then you *should* be here; your luck has taken you here, to the *Funakoshi*. You cannot doubt it. You have lost your home, perhaps your family, but think about whether or not you have found something else." Ahm Baqa paused, as if searching for the right words.

"We have studied this question of luck ourselves," Baqa said, still in his gentlest tone. "The trouble is that it is not predictable. The real question is, by what standards does this luck proceed? What tells your inborn luck just what is best for you? Why, for example, did you take the test at all—why did your luck not find for you a way out of taking it? Why did your luck *let* you be separated from your family and your world? We must presume that it is for your long-range interests, but no one knows what those interests are. Luck, but what kind of luck? We do not know, and the Emperor does not know. That is why he is so afraid of it.

"Kid, if you trust it, this luck of yours, then trust in us, and we will see to it that the Guard never finds you. You can wait with us, to discover just where your luck is leading you."

"The trouble is that I don't trust it," Paul said dumbly, his despair gone. He had nothing to hide anymore; this man knew everything already.

Still, in a corner of his mind, a paranoiac doubt remained.

"Of course you do not trust it," Baqa said animatedly. "It is too new, your knowledge of it. And so you do not trust us." He paused, lost in thought.

Then he did something which caused Paul's heart to leap into his throat, and all his doubts to surge forward again.

Baqa flipped his right wrist, and all at once, the muzzle of a finger blaster was in Paul's face.

"Normally," Baqa said, "I would not allow someone as young as you to handle a weapon like this. But, if nothing else, your luck should prevent any serious accidents with it. Maybe also your common sense, I do not know. So that you can trust us, so that you can see that we hold no threat over you, I am giving you this." And he placed the blaster in Paul's open palm, where it nestled like a deadly stone.

Paul looked at it, flabbergasted. He had never held one before, and knew that it was not only illegal, but impossibly expensive. He looked up at Ahm Baqa, and encountered again those disconcerting, direct, coal-black eyes. Wordlessly, Paul slid the blaster into his sleeve, where it disappeared as if it had been hidden there forever.

"Come, what is your name?" Ahm Baqa said softly.

"Paul Cartier," Paul said.

CHAPTER 11

Paul was led by Shimmy down the corridors of the circus ship to a small cabin, little more than a cubbyhole.

"This is yours," Shimmy said. "Mine is across the hall. If you need anything, just ask."

"Thanks," Paul said. He looked around the cabin, then back at Shimmy expectantly.

"Dinner is in an hour—I'll take you there myself," Shimmy said. "Then we each do some maintenance work around the ship, and after that everyone who is able goes to a k'rati class. Baqa told me that that includes you."

"K'rati class," Paul said. "What's that?"

"You'll find out soon enough," the red-haired boy said, not unkindly.

Suddenly Paul noticed the blond youth, Jonny, lounging in the doorway of a cabin just a few steps down from
his own.

"Hi," Paul said tentatively.

The other said nothing. He continued lounging, as if
Paul wasn't there.

Shimmy smiled. "Don't pay any attention to Jonny,"
he said, "he's always like this." With that, Shimmy
launched an incredibly fast kick at Jonny's head. With an
angular motion resembling a swat, Jonny knocked it
effortlessly away, scarcely moving at all. He did not smile.

Shimmy chuckled. He tossed his red hair, and said to
Paul: "See you in an hour." He disappeared into his own
cabin.

Glancing at the blond-haired boy, Paul hesitated. But
he could think of nothing to do or say. He ducked
through his own doorway and into the cabin.

A wide shelf ran along one wall—it took Paul a full
minute to realize that this was the bed. It held an old-
fashioned liquid mattress no more than five centimeters
thick, inflated to its full capacity. The effect was one of
hard but yielding rubber. Paul poked at it tentatively,
and it scarcely sagged beneath the linen coverlet.

Adjacent to the head of the bed was a tiny, built-in
desk. There was a shelf above it, on which rested a pile of
reading disks. Curious, Paul selected one, and popped it
into the desk reader. The letters of the first page floated
into view on the surface of the desk, as if they were
etched there. Paul read: "Fragments of the Ancient Esoteric Traditions, vol. 23: Discussions in Advaita Ve-
danta." Puzzled, Paul read a few lines, but they made no

sense at all to him. Anyway, he had no notion of what "esoteric" meant.

There were washroom facilities in what had first appeared to be a closet, with the usual composting toilet and washstand. Another closet held a few plain work clothes, with a laundry chute. There was one unusual garment, a dead-white buttonless, wide-sleeved shirt with long tails and a wide, white belt, and a loose-fitting pair of pants. Paul couldn't see any loops on the pants for the belt to pass through; the pants had a drawstring, and otherwise was featureless. Paul fingered the strange garment briefly, and then passed on.

There was nothing else in the room. Paul sat heavily on the bed, and wondered what was coming next.

Already, he had an ambivalent feeling about these people. Shimmy was nice enough, Jonny not so nice. Ahm Baqa puzzled him completely; he seemed to change moods from moment to moment, with a constant fiery intensity like some kind of video hero.

Yet Paul was inclined to trust him, and he could see no flaw in the logic that the mustached man had placed before him. Indeed, Baqa could have turned him in on Elsinore, and had not. And—he touched his sleeve—he had the finger blaster.

Paul imagined what was going on right now, in the upper reaches of the ship. Baqa would be reporting to the Captain—whoever that was—and they would be discussing his case. Perhaps the Captain would prefer to take no chances, but to call in the Imperial Guard. Perhaps not. Paul decided wearily that he would have to trust his luck on that—he had detected no deviousness in Baqa's manner, but he would have to keep his guard up, all the same.

Paul looked out into the corridor, and there was Jonny, sagging in the doorframe next door. Paul frowned.

"What are you, a guard or something?" he demanded. The other did not move, did not even look up. Paul ducked back into his cabin, and tried to puzzle it all out.

When Shimmy came for him, Paul had resigned himself to follow along, while at the same time keeping a careful watch on things. He did not want to cause any trouble, but he was not taking any chances either.

Shimmy led Paul to an immense dining hall, with Jonny trailing along behind. There were long rows of tables, with all the circus complement crammed together. It was cafeteria style—the three of them stood in line before a long counter, and filled up trays of the plain food that was arrayed before them.

There were many greens, a surprising amount in view of their bulk and perishability. By the time Paul had gone the length of the counter, his tray was piled with vegetables and fruits, most of them familiar enough, a few very strange indeed.

He looked in vain for meat, but there was none to be had.

Shimmy elbowed his way onto the end of a table, and pulled Paul down beside him. Paul found himself the center of attraction for a dozen diverse strangers. He glanced hurriedly around at the array of faces, and then turned to his place and ate hungrily. The rest of the table resumed their meal.

After a time, Paul's pace slowed, as his starving body began to fill. Jonny was nowhere to be seen. He looked around, and saw that some of the people did not hesitate to fill their trays a second and third time. Paul got up and selected a number of things that he had particularly liked. He sat down next to Shimmy, and said:

"Shimmy, how come there's no meat?" The rest of the table broke off their conversations and looked at him, amused.

"Sonny, what do we need with meat?" an older man said. Paul scanned the group, but he could detect no hostility, only a simple curiosity.

"Well," Paul said, "for the protein, I guess."

A heavily built woman said, "Oh, there's plenty of protein in what you're eating, don't worry about that."

The swarthy man added: "Anyway, meat's expensive. Why feed a cow the same stuff you can feed yourself?"

A little nettled, Paul snapped: "Yeah? Do you eat grass too?"

The table rocked with laughter. The swarthy man said:

"Well, you've got a point, sonny, but we do eat wheat, rye, corn, and a lot of other grasses. But tell me, sonny . . . can you turn your tongue upside down?"

Paul's mouth dropped open in astonishment. The older man leaned over, as if to peer inside.

"Wha . . . ?" Paul managed to say, before clamping his jaw shut.

"I can," the swarthy man said. "Watch." And he stuck his tongue out, and to Paul's outraged surprise, it was upside down!

Desperately he turned to Shimmy, who said, looking at the bigger man:

"Big deal, Lyle. Let's see you pat your head and make a circle on your stomach at the same time."

"I can't believe this," Paul said loudly. But Lyle was

patting his head with one hand, and trying to make a circle on his stomach with the other. The only trouble was, that his hand insisted on patting his stomach in rhythm with his other hand.

Frowning, Lyle switched arms. The same thing happened. Then he tried making a circle on his head, and sure enough, his other hand started making a circle on his stomach.

But when he tried to make his head hand pat, his stomach hand started patting too.

The silence, which had been rising in a high tension around the table, exploded suddenly into whoops and guffaws and howls. Paul regarded his new companions incredulously, as if he were looking into a gathering of lunatics.

"Wait, wait," Shimmy shouted. The noise faded.

"Now watch," he said.

Then, gravely, he brought his right hand up and patted his head. And he brought his left hand over, and made a circle on his stomach.

The crowd cheered. Shimmy bowed deliberately, a wide grin on his lips.

Paul found himself patting his head. He brought himself up short.

"So what does that prove, you red-haired deviate?" the older man demanded, laughing. "Let's see you do this."

He wiggled his ears. By thunder, he wiggled them as if there were strings tied onto them, being pulled by somebody across the room!

"Oh, no," Shimmy said. "You know very well, Sven, that I can't do that. But Vera here can bend her fingers back to her wrist. Show him, Vera."

Vera was the heavily built woman. She matter-of-factly grabbed her left index finger with her right hand, and bent it backward until it grazed the skin on her wrist.

"Ouch," Sven said. "If I tried that, you'd hear a loud cracking noise."

"And a loud screaming one," Shimmy added.

"Look, somebody please tell me," Paul said plaintively. "What does all this prove?"

There was silence for a moment, as everyone at the table looked at Paul.

It was Sven who finally said:

"Nothing much. It's just that some things are more or less hereditary, rather than learned. *I* can't bend my fingers like that to save my life. My parents probably couldn't either. But at least one of them, or their parents, could wiggle their ears. Or maybe there was a mutation that produced me."

"That's it, that's got to be it," Shimmy yelled. "You're too weird to be anything else!"

"Well, what about your friend here," Sven demanded. "Is luck learned, or is it hereditary, or is he a mutant too?"

The table laughed again. Paul paled. He sat still as ice, looking at the strange faces before him.

"Sven, you must be lucky at ear-wiggling," said Vera, and they laughed again.

Paul dragged Shimmy into the corridor and faced him, trembling.

"You mean *they know everything about me?*" he demanded. He felt betrayed by Ahm Baqa, surrounded by a hundred potential spies.

Shimmy said, "It's pretty hard to keep a secret in a group like this." Paul groaned and rolled his eyes back.

"No!" he said. "What will happen when we land on Shad? With these blabbermouths, the whole planet will know inside of a week."

Shimmy laughed, and Paul looked at him incredulously. Then Shimmy grabbed his arm.

"Listen," he said seriously, "don't worry about it. Every one of these people hates the Guard as much as you do. Look!" he said, and pointing at the heavy woman at their table. "Vera there is wanted on sixteen planets for tax refusal and 'abusing' the Imperial Guard. Sven was a forger, and the Guard would give a hundred thousand marks to catch him. Are you going to give them away?"

Paul admitted that he would not.

"Well, then, you can assume that they won't give you away, either. By the time you've spent a month on this ship, you'll know so many tales about these people that you'll be a walking time bomb for them. They won't betray you, if only because they don't want you to betray them. And that includes me." He glared at Paul, whose feelings were subsiding.

"You?" he said wonderingly. "You're barely older than I am. What could the Guard want you for?"

"You'll find that out from someone else. Come on, it's time to do some work."

Wordlessly, Paul followed him down the corridor.

Paul spent the next two hours cleaning a solar collector panel which had been brought in from outside the ship. Most of the ship's power came from these panels; since the ship was always relatively near a sun, it was the cheapest form of energy available. The ship turned to the comparatively wasteful nuclear power only when out of range of sufficient sunlight, which almost never happened, or when the collectors were damaged or dirty.

Most ships, Paul knew, had automatic devices to take care of such cleaning chores, but the *Funakoshi* was such an old relic that it lacked such conveniences. "Costs money for parts and such," was Shimmy's taciturn answer to Paul's inquiry. "Anyway, there's nothing much else to do in deep space, so we might as well do something useful."

The job over, Shimmy brought him back to his cabin. "It's almost time for the k'rati class," he said. "Put on your 'gi' and we'll go down to the gym."

" 'Gi'?" Paul said. "What's that?"

"It's the white thing in your closet. Put it on and I'll meet you out here."

Paul put it on. The thing was strange and bulky. He stuffed the tails down the pants, and tied them with the drawstring. He wrapped the belt around it all and made a knot. Using a strap built into the weapon, he carefully secured the finger blaster to his upper arm (for the sleeves of the "gi" were disconcertingly open and short).

Shimmy broke into a gale of uproarious laughter when he saw him.

"No, no," he said, when he could catch his breath. "You wear it this way, like mine."

Paul saw at once the logic of it, although it looked a little strange. He pulled his shirttails out, and tied the pants up under them with the drawstring. Then he looped the white belt around his waist, and tied it in front of him with a square knot.

He noticed that Shimmy's belt was brown, and began to ask him why. But then Jonny came out of his room, and Shimmy led them down the corridor. Jonny's belt was also brown, Paul noted.

They arrived at the gym, and Paul saw that it was crowded with people doing exercises of one form or another. "Come on, limber up," Shimmy said, and began to stretch his arms and legs. Paul tried to follow suit.

All at once a hush came over the assembly. Paul looked up, and saw Ahm Baqa walking into the gym. He too wore a "gi," but his belt was scarlet. Paul looked around, seeing a rainbow of colors on the various "gi's," but no others that were scarlet.

They all lined up. (Shimmy whispered, "You have to stand at the far end of the line. Just do everything that the person next to you does.") Paul stood awkwardly next to a young woman with a yellow belt, and wondered what was going on.

There was a brief, unintelligible command from Baqa, who was facing the center of the line, and they all knelt. Another command, and everyone closed their eyes, Paul glancing nervously around before following suit. There was a long period of silence, in which Paul's mind whirled with questions and confusion. Then another command, and Paul's eyes snapped open to find everyone bowing to the floor. Paul had scarcely dipped before they suddenly leaped to their feet.

A woman with a black belt came from the head of the line—Paul saw that it was Vera, the heavy-set woman from the cafeteria. As Baqa stood aside, she began to lead them all in a series of loosening exercises.

At first, Paul looked at everyone curiously, while trying to imitate them. But soon, he began to pay more attention to his body, which was protesting vehemently at the unusual treatment.

They did stretching exercises, deep knee bends, push-ups, sit-ups, leg lifts, side straddle hops, twisting exercises, and a dozen things Paul could not name. He thought, between gasps of fatigue, of the incongruity of it, a shipload of circus people lined up like soldiers, following the commands of a fat woman. He had never heard of anything like this.

Finally, when he could scarcely hold his body upright, they stopped. The crowd broke into groups, depending on belt color. Paul stood alone for a moment, until he saw Jonny heading toward him. He stiffened.

"I've got to show you the basics," Jonny said sourly. "So you just do what I do, and you won't get hurt."

"Wait a minute," Paul said desperately, "what is all this? What's the point of it?"

Jonny looked at Paul as if he were a moron. "Sh'tok'n k'rati," he said coldly. "You're going to learn it and learn it good. Now stand like this." He demonstrated a square stance, with the left leg in the lead, knee over the toes, while the right leg stretched back straight, the foot only slightly turned outward.

Paul tried it. He asked:

"At least tell me what it's for." Jonny reached out and adjusted Paul's upper body so that it rode straight over the stance, stomach slightly out.

"What do you think it's for, you idiot," he growled, not

taking his eyes off Paul's stance. "Stiffen your back leg—
if I push you, it shouldn't even budge."

He pushed Paul violently, and Paul fell backward
onto the floor.

"See?" he said tauntingly. "Do it right, and that won't
happen."

Paul felt anger well in him. He leaped up, and threw
a savage punch at Jonny's head.

Jonny slapped it away as if it were a fly.

"Don't be stupid," he began. But Paul was swinging
with the other arm, all of his self-control gone.

This time, the block was bone-jarring. Paul winced,
and drew back his other hand for a swing. Off-handedly,
almost detachedly, Jonny's foot flew off the floor and
buried itself in Paul's stomach.

His breath went out in a whoosh. He fell backward on
the floor, and doubled up, gasping. For a moment, he
could not catch his breath.

"Now you see, you jerk?" Jonny said, standing over
him. "K'rati is self-defense. Once you know it, you don't
have to take this from me."

"I . . . I . . . ," Paul gasped, "I . . . don't have . . .
to . . . take . . . it . . . NOW!" He reached out and
pulled Jonny's left leg out from under him.

Jonny lost his balance. But as he fell backward, he
whipped his right foot out, and clipped Paul along the
side of the face with the edge of his foot. Jonny landed on
his back, his arms slapping down to absorb the impact.
He held his head close to his chest, so that it would not
bounce off the floor.

The blow dazed Paul, but he climbed to his feet. But

just barely. Jonny swept his left foot in an arc, and kicked Paul's feet from under him. Paul landed with a thud. All of his reason was now gone. He lurched to a kneeling crouch, and reached for the finger blaster.

Jonny kicked it out of his hand, and his fist crashed against the side of Paul's head. Paul barely felt the blow, consciousness went so suddenly.

Paul woke up in his cabin, to find Ahm Baqa standing over him. Jonny stood rigidly in the background, his face without expression.

Paul's head throbbed. He sat up and groaned.

"How are you?" Baqa asked.

"I've felt better," Paul said, bringing his hands to his head. He winced as his hand found a lump there.

"Now," said Baqa, "do you know what k'rati is?" His voice sounded amused. Paul was not.

"Yes, I wish you'd told me earlier," he said angrily. "It's illegal combat." He began to look at Baqa, but stopped as his sore muscles protested.

"Of course it is illegal," Baqa said. "What does it matter if generations of Earth people practiced it without overthrowing their governments? Our Emperor, he takes no chances." He scowled at Paul. "And now, should you not have something to say to Jonny?"

"*Me* have something to say!" Paul exclaimed. His whole body felt like a single bruised mass.

"Yes, you," Baqa said. "Look back on that fight. Is there anything that bothers you about it?"

They waited five minutes while Paul's mind and pride

resisted the suggestion. But finally his reason took hold, and he knew that he had to say it.

"You're right," he said, subdued. "I went out of my head. I never should have drawn the blaster, no matter what was happening." With a start, he felt the blaster nestled against his forearm. They had returned it to him!

"As a matter of fact," he said, looking up at Jonny, despite the pain. "I should not have attacked you in the first place. I'm sorry." And he let his head fall again. No emotion had crossed over Jonny's face at all.

There was a moment of silence, and then Paul heard Baqa say something to Jonny. There was another moment of silence, and then he heard Jonny's voice.

"And I'm sorry. That last blow that put you out—I shouldn't have done it. I lost my head too, and that's something a k'ratika should never do. When I saw that blaster, I almost killed you."

Paul looked at him again, and saw nothing written on the blond face. It was as if he was reciting a lesson.

Baqa said: "I can punish Jonny for this, and indeed, I already have, in the k'rati class." Paul could see no evidence of it, but he saw Jonny wince.

He never found out what the punishment had been.

"As he said, someone who knows Sh'tok'n k'rati as well as he does should not lose control. But I cannot very well punish you, until you understand what is expected of you, on the k'rati floor. Shimmy will tell you everything, before the next class.

"For now, think about it all, Paul. If you do nothing at all in your life, rid yourself of your temper absolutely. Never do anything in anger; do everything only because it needs to be done."

With that statement, Baqa turned and walked out.

Paul regarded Jonny, as the latter stood there. Then, without a word, Jonny too left.

And Paul was alone with his pain and his guilt.

CHAPTER 12

Planetfall.

The bronze planet Shad stretched out below the starship. Paul gazed at it through the observation screen in the *Funakoshi*'s stern, and was captivated. Many times had he seen the scene on the video, but never had he guessed the grandeur of the real thing!

It had been the return of the finger blaster, more than anything else, that had convinced Paul of Ahm Baqa's integrity. In light of Paul's irresponsible use of it, the return of it was astonishing.

He had been on the *Funakoshi* nearly forty-eight hours now, and he was beginning to understand, if only a little bit, the character of the motley and complicated crew.

The society that the circus had created was strange and wonderful to him. Paul marveled at the rigid discipline of the k'rati class, a discipline not at all evident outside the class itself. Nothing, not the mild compulsions of skool, nor later, the erratic, stiff behavior of the Imperial Guard, had prepared Paul for it. He felt that the two-hour daily submersion in the complete obedience of the class had left an indelible stamp on the character of the crew, yet he could not put his finger on just how. Outside of the class, they all seemed irreverent and almost scatter-brained, as if in contrast with the iron of that strange art called k'rati.

He looked down on Shad with fascination tinged with apprehension. There lay a world of marvels perhaps, but there also lay the Imperial Guard. Paul knew the technical skills of the Guard, and knew that by this time, jumper satellites could easily have transferred the alarm to all the planets of the Three Hundred Suns. The Guard could not suspect that Paul had even left Elsinore, and yet they would take no chances, he knew. Even now, he was sure, they were waiting for him on Shad.

The planet cast a yellow-brown glow onto Paul's face as he gazed through the screen. It seemed to be all land, with no water at all. Paul had heard that it was the metallic vegetation which gave Shad its distinctive color, and that the planet was by no means as arid as it appeared from a distance.

Here and there he saw storm clouds; he knew that the water which they cast down was hidden by the vegetation, and that far from being a desert, Shad was actually covered with a blanket of dank, nearly impenetrable jungle. It was one of the most common of all Shad's plants which produced that beautiful, golden fabric that was so highly prized. Nevertheless, Paul knew that it was a poor planet, and the *Funakoshi* foresaw only a brief stay there.

Ahm Baqa came up behind him.

"Come," he said, "we must prepare you for the landing."

"The Guard will be waiting for me," Paul said.

"Yes," said Baqa. Paul trailed after him down a long corridor into the depths of the ship. "And so you must be disguised," Baqa said. "In here."

Paul was surprised to see a modern laboratory open up before him.

"We have made the Guard believe that we need these facilities for our animals, to prepare their many diverse kinds of food and medicines," Baqa said. "Actually, we make many other uses of it."

Deftly, the ship's doctor (Paul was surprised to find that it was Lyle, the well-muscled, swarthy man he had seen in the cafeteria), molded a paper-thin, transparent sheath for Paul's hands and feet. In an instant, his fingerprints and toeprints were altered.

Then, to Paul's discomfort, he was placed in a surgical chair, and something was inserted deep into his throat. When the procedure was completed, Paul said irritably:

"What was that all about?" He stopped suddenly. His voice had an unfamiliar rasp to it, as if it belonged to someone else. He looked disbelievingly up at Ahm Baqa.

Baqa smiled. "Now your old voiceprint will not match the new one. The device is easily inserted and withdrawn, so do not worry about permanent effects."

The doctor molded Paul's hairline with a razor, and cropped his longish brown hair. He did something with a flesh-colored plastic around Paul's ears and nose, and spent some time working on his cheekbone.

Paul was astonished at the result. With his hairline different, his nose was suddenly squatter, and his face squarer. The resemblance to his old self was uncomfortably small.

"It's a confounded nuisance," Lyle said irritably. "We may have to go through this every planetfall." He looked inquiringly at Ahm Baqa. "Or else we could fix him . . . permanently . . ."

Baqa waved him away. "We will do it every time if we have to," he said coldly. "As to the other idea, it is entirely up to Paul. I will not ask him to decide until he knows us much better than he does now."

"And what about a brain scanner?" the doctor snapped. "How are you fixing to disguise his brain waves so that they don't match his old pattern?"

Baqa frowned. Paul gasped; he said: "Now hold on. What are you planning to do, brain surgery? You can forget it!" He glared at the two men, who looked at him bemusedly.

"Actually, Paul," Baqa said, "we could alter your brain pattern surgically with no change in your personality, IQ or anything else. However," he went on, ignoring Paul's building anger, "I will again leave that entirely up to you. If you should decide to stay with us, then you can consider it. For now, we will hope that the Guard will not employ a brain scanner, and trust to the simpler methods of identification."

"And if they don't?" Paul demanded. He knew enough about the Guard now to take nothing for granted.

"And if they do not," Baqa said quietly, "there are

82

other ways." And there was nothing Paul could do to get him to explain further.

The planet loomed until it filled the entire viewing screen, like a ruddy orange floating in a sea of ink. Paul watched the clouds loom up and seem to spread apart as the *Funakoshi* soundlessly descended.

The landing was disconcertingly rough, which Paul had not expected. Apparently the scenes which he had seen on video were of ships considerably newer than this hulk.

Like a beehive, the *Funakoshi* swarmed into activity. Baqa ordered Paul to remain at his side, and Paul obeyed. Baqa oversaw the unloading of the ship, the long procession of wagons which carried the circus to the fairgrounds. Thus Paul saw passing before him the entire melange of people, animals and things that made the *Funakoshi* circus what it was.

There were common workers, both men and women, who put up the circus at each stop and administered to it and later took it down. Paul knew a few of them from the k'rati class, and liked them all. There were the trainers, who dealt with the ofttime savage and unpredictable beasts from the Three Hundred Suns. And there were the carnival barkers, whom Paul liked less, perhaps because of their glibness and ready wit that were too fast for him.

Ahm Baqa acted as foreman, yet Paul rarely saw any actual use of his authority. It was not so much that the crew did what he said without question, but that they and Baqa were invariably in agreement over the course to be followed. It was as if the experience of k'rati had turned all their thoughts in the same direction; or probably more to the point, it had fostered in them an objectivity of thought whose conclusions were always the same.

And there was the "Captain." It had not taken Paul long to discover that Baqa was by no means the supreme commander here. Instead, the "Captain" was a sort of commission of three, who made decisions by consensus; Baqa was only one.

Paul failed to see what earthshaking decisions there were to be made—perhaps what planet to go to next, and keeping the circus solvent. What else was there?

One of the other two commissioners was a woman of about thirty. Paul learned to his astonishment that she was the titular owner of the *Funakoshi,* although Baqa had added that in reality, "the ship belongs to all of us."

She was also the navigator, who kept track of the jump coordinates. On a starship, this was perhaps the most important job, for an error of only a decimal point could cause them to jump into an entirely unfamiliar region of space. Countless starships had been lost over the centuries, until the intricacies of the interspace coordinate system had been mastered at last.

The woman's name was Sylva—Paul saw her pass by now, among the disembarking crew. She was auburn-haired, and thin, as if the navigating responsibility weighed too heavily on her shoulders. But Paul had seen her in the k'rati class, and she wore a belt that was black, with a single crimson stripe. No one else ranked higher than she did in that class, with the exception of Ahm Baqa.

The third commissioner was also a woman, but Paul had never seen her. She was Aliyah, and she was old. It was said that a sickness kept her confined to the ship, and she was rarely taken from her cabin. Yet she was universally respected, and there was a place for her in the k'rati line, next to Sylva.

With Baqa, Paul climbed on the last wagon in the line. All of the hundred or so crew members were before him, sitting by ones and twos on the primitive circus wagons, except for the three left behind to maintain the starship and Aliyah.

Paul looked up into the copper sky of Shad, and the heat seemed to wrap him in a humid shroud. Somewhere up ahead, the griff screamed uncannily, raising the hackles of all who could hear it.

"Shad is a provincial, suspicious planet," Baqa said to Paul out of the corner of his mouth. "The Guard is kind here; no one thinks to question its control or its wisdom. Shad I have never liked; the people here do no thinking on their own, but frame their thoughts so that they agree with the propaganda of authority." Paul guessed that the climate had something to do with it. At a constant ninety-eight degrees, all of the outside work needed to harvest the cantankerous fiber plant (despite the most modern machinery) would weigh one down in sweat and fatigue. The gravity pulled a little heavier than it did on Elsinore.

An insect descended on Paul's leg and took a tiny, piercing bite before he slapped it away. Shad—he could think of little to recommend it.

The wagons moved in fits and starts. Baqa frowned at the controls, and seemed deep in thought. Normally he would have been at the front of the procession, and would already know what was holding it up. Paul felt a little guilty, but was glad that Baqa was there.

The Shad spaceport was considerably smaller than the one on Elsinore. Paul could see no more than a dozen starships arrayed in it, most of them bulky cargo ships whose purpose here was obvious. Here and there were the obligatory Guard ships, needlenosed giants of power and speed. They could outrun the *Funakoshi* as if the latter were standing still, and outjump her with no trouble at all.

Ahead they could see that the wagons were passing through some sort of gate or guardpost. Paul strained, and could see that the Guard was there, scanning the wagons with the same sort of heat sensor that they had used on him on Elsinore. But there was something else; the drivers of the wagons were climbing down from them and entering the guardhouse, to reemerge several minutes later and drive on.

The check was to be more thorough, this time.

"Keep as close to me as you can," Baqa said suddenly, rousing Paul from the fears that were growing in his mind. "Remember that you are disguised and that your identification characteristics have been changed. They will check the crewmen left in the ship soon enough; one way or another you would be checked, and we might as well get it over with here, as anywhere else."

His tone was grim. Nevertheless, Paul felt reassured. He sat up straighter on the wagon, looking at the copper Shadian sky.

All at once, it was their wagon that had arrived at the guardhouse. A tall, swarthy Guardsman motioned them down from the wagon and into the building. Dumbly Paul followed Ahm Baqa, who strode through the door.

Inside it was obvious what was going on. Paul recognized the machines at once. Fingerprints, voiceprints, and . . . *brain waves!*

Baqa surveyed the equipment with a scowl, and announced loudly:

"Ahm Baqa, Ringmaster; and my son Asa, just returned from the Explorers out of Pangborn."

Paul gasped. Surely the Guard would see through this clumsy story! Why, the moment that he placed his hand on the fingerprint scanner, the fact that there was no record for him in the Empire's data banks would be immediately known. What good would the phony fingerprints do him then? At the very least, he would be held until his identity was verified, and this, Paul knew, could not end in his favor.

He looked frantically at Baqa, but the latter seemed completely unperturbed. "Asa, you go first," he boomed, looking back at him.

Paul hesitated. He could see no way out, but hung back nonetheless.

And the Explorers! Paul had heard of them, of course, the unofficial training ground for children whose crazy parents wanted something more for them than the traditional skool. They accompanied those madmen who made it their business to jump over unconfirmed coordinates to see what lay on the other side. They were the ones who discovered new worlds for the Three Hundred Suns Empire, and with frightful regularity, many did not return.

Naturally the Emperor tolerated them. No Guardsman or ships were wasted in that risky business, and all the benefits of discovery were the Empire's in the end.

Always Paul had considered the Explorers fools, and

now all of a sudden here he was! And more than that: Paul knew that the identity of every Explorer was well noted in the data base.

Paul's head spun, almost in pain. And besides all this, there was the brain scanner!

He looked frantically at Ahm Baqa, but the latter seemed absolutely unmoved.

Paul half turned to run. Ahm Baqa reached out and grabbed him by the arm, propelling him forward.

Gasping, Paul felt pain lance through his upper arm, like the jab of a needle. To his horror, he felt volition leave him, and his mind became trapped in a body that would not, could not, respond to his commands.

Like an automaton he moved forward and thrust his hand into the fingerprint scanner. The Guardsman behind the central console watched him suspiciously. Then he studied the screen before him, where the ID readout would appear.

The Guardsman watched for a moment, and then said: "All right, you check out. Move on to the voice printer."

What?! Paul's numbed brain shouted. Check out? Impossible!

Again his body moved without his asking it to. He resisted it, to no avail. His thoughts were getting fuzzy, and he fought frantically to keep some kind of control.

"Repeat after me," came the mechanical tones of the voice scanner. "'Often have I crawled through the purple swamp before.'"

Paul heard his own voice come, through an increasing whirl of confusion.

"Often have I crawled through the purple swamp before!"

Another pause. Paul's body did nothing as his mind raved.

"Check," the Guardsman said.

Dumbly, Paul's body moved to the brain scanner.

No, no, no! his mind screamed. Keep away from it, don't go near it!

His body sat down heavily on the scanner chair. The cap was placed over his head.

It's the end, he thought, panic-stricken. Through a gray haze, he saw Ahm Baqa watching him unemotionally, as if from a long distance.

Betrayer! his mind screamed. Betrayer!

"Check!" the Guardsman called out.

Paul sat there emptily, his mind barely functioning at all. Then, without his command, his body stood up, and moved toward the outside door.

"Say, what is ailing you, Asa?" Baqa said, reaching out to steady him with his hand. Again, but this time from far away, Paul felt a pain lance through his arm.

"You know," Baqa said to the Guardsmen, "I think that the heat is getting to him. Let me put him on the wagon, and then you can run the check on me."

"Not necessary," the Guardsman behind the console said coldly. "We're not looking for a bald-headed circus clown like you."

As if he had not heard the insult, Baqa guided Paul out the door and onto the wagon. He threw it into motion, and they left the guardhouse behind.

Paul groaned, and bent forward over his knees. His head was clearing, bathed in a confused, crimson fire.

What, he wondered, had happened to him? His body twitched as if with the ague. He was sweating a cold, viscous sweat.

At length, he straightened, the discomfort tugging at him. He looked at Baqa with pain in his eyes, in silent inquiry.

Baqa looked at him soberly.

"How . . ." Paul began. Baqa silenced him with a gesture.

"Look at the palm of my hand," he ordered. "Look at it!"

He opened it, and Paul looked. Nestled in the palm was a tiny sac, from which thrust a slender, short needle. Paul stared at it dopily, not altogether grasping what it was.

"It held a mind drug," Baqa said. "I drugged you for the brain scanner, and I administered the antidote the same way, with the other hand. The drug caused your brain pattern to become other than it usually is. It caused it to conform with that of Asa Baqa in the data bank."

"Asa Baqa?" Paul said, almost gibbering. His mind skipped around, and he waited for it to quiet down.

"The antidote had to come within five minutes," Baqa said gravely. "The drug itself would have caused you to start raving by that time, and the Guard would be on your back."

Blast the antidote, Paul thought. His mind would not quit jumping, and he wanted to steady it down.

"Why didn't you tell me?" he asked in an agonized tone of voice. "Why didn't you prepare me for it?" He looked at Baqa, the pain behind his eyes.

"I could not," Baqa said gently. "The drug acts upon

your will. It is the last suggestion that you hear that determines what your body does for the succeeding five minutes. If I had warned you, who knows what thoughts would be passing through your mind at the last minute? As it was, you did just what the setting called for, and that is what we wanted."

"But ASA BAQA!" Paul yelled. "There is no Asa Baqa! How could there be a record in that data bank? Why did the Guard pass me through without a record?"

"How do you know that there is no Asa Baqa?" the mustached man said irritably. "You got through, did you not? What more do you want?"

Paul felt the rebuke like a blow. Here he was, questioning the decisions that had probably saved his life!

Then the thought of his luck came to him again, and he wondered arrogantly if he needed anyone at all to protect him, if his luck would carry him through no matter what. The idea brought courage back to him, and he faced Baqa once again.

"I know you probably saved my life back there," he said shrilly, "but I must know if there is an Asa Baqa, and how his brain wave pattern could possibly match mine, even under a mind drug." He glared at Baqa with such stern indignation that Baqa laughed, and clapped him painfully on the back.

"All right, you little warrior, if it makes you feel better, the drug makes *everyone's* brain pattern look the same, something that the Guard has apparently not yet realized. And as far as Asa Baqa is concerned, we inserted his records into the data bank by microwave as the *Funakoshi* descended on Shad. Highly illegal, of course, but anyone with the necessary technology can do it.

There is much more to the *Funakoshi* than meets the eye.

"One more thing," he said, turning on Paul. "Perhaps you think that your luck carried you through this, and that it will carry you through anything else. Listen to me and listen well. You cannot count on it for anything! Get it out of your head that it gives you a free ride.

"Look at what has happened to you: you were torn from your family and your home planet, thrown into a crate with the most savage being in the Three Hundred Suns, manhandled by a group of strangers, and knocked unconscious in your first k'rati confrontation.

"Tell me this, Paul: when does your luck act, and when not? What destiny does it have for you? Power? Money? Love? Does it want you to be a dictator or a martyr? A soldier or a poet or a sage? Or maybe just healthy and alive? You tell me, Paul: where can you trust it so much that you abandon your own skills, your own effort, your own knowledge and experience?"

Chastened, Paul looked away, at the poverty-ridden streets of Shad. Beggars wandered there, and ragged children, brown from the merciless sun.

Finally, he spoke softly:

"Tell me," he said, ". . . is there an Asa Baqa?"

Ahm Baqa looked moodily ahead, his black eyes filming over.

"What does it matter?" he said at last.

CHAPTER 13

"Asa! Asa Baqa!"

Startled, Paul looked up. About a hundred meters away, standing among some game wagons, was Shimmy, waving in Paul's direction. It took Paul a moment to realize that he was waving at him.

"News travels fast," Paul muttered to himself. He waved perfunctorily, and walked toward the red-haired boy.

Ahm Baqa had dismissed Paul with a curt: "Go into the fairway; there is work to be done." Paul had wandered about briefly, watching the workers raise the tents and put up booths. He wanted to see the animal wagons, but they were somewhere up ahead.

"All right, *Asa,*" said Shimmy, drawling out the last word with ill-concealed delight. "Here's what I want you to do."

Paul became an assistant to a carnival barker named Ludwig. The latter was a big, blond man of herculean dimension. He had a jovial, enticing way about him, and their booth did rather well, considering the slim pickings on Shad.

It was a primitive setup, nothing more than a game of darts. If the customer broke four red balloons in a row, the customer won a prize—the oldtime Kewpie doll. Other scores got lesser prizes. But Ludwig made a true game of it, moving his huge bulk with the grace of a dancer around the booth as he cajoled, razzed, praised, cheered, and bantered with his patrons.

Paul had a tough time keeping up. His job was to fill the balloons from a compressor and attach them to the target board. It was fun for a while.

Around midnight, after the circus was closed, they all headed for the ship. They ate, slept, and upon waking up in the morning, entered upon a rigorous two-hour k'rati class. Often Paul was so tired and sore that he could barely move when it came time to return to the carnival booth. But return he did, and worked. "Asa," Shimmy had said, "there's no point wasting your wake-up energy on work. We use it for more important things."

Everyone now called him Asa, as if the name Paul had suddenly disappeared. He found himself responding freely to it, and sometimes he caught himself thinking as "Asa Baqa."

Rarely did he see his "father," Ahm Baqa, save in the class and once on the fairway. To his annoyance, the carnival booths were outside of the circus proper, and he saw nothing of what went on inside the big tent, where Ahm Baqa was ringmaster.

It was the third night that Paul saw Baqa on the fairway. The mustached man came directly to him during a lull in the carnival action. Paul blinked at the man's ringmaster regalia, an opulent array of sequins and velvet.

Ahm Baqa took Paul aside.

"Asa, I have a bit of news that concerns you." Paul was struck by a note of concern in the big man's voice. "Our sources tell us that the Emperor has sent out a specialist in locating runaways, a Finder with thirty years experience and an uncanny sixth sense about such things. And the Executioner may be with him as well.

"Whether they will come to Shad my sources do not know; in fact, they do not know what the Finder looks like; but they know that he exists, and is after you. Be on your guard, and keep the blaster at your hand at all times. But do not use it if you can avoid it—it would be a sure giveaway as to where you are, and your cover would be at an end."

All Paul had time to do was nod, and then Baqa was gone.

Paul had never heard of the Finder. But of the Executioner he had heard only too much.

He protected the Emperor from attack, it was said. He could put his bare fist through a brick wall. He could crush rocks in his hand. He was someone that boys admired and men feared. He was the most renowned weapons-master in the Three Hundred Suns. And already in his brief time with the *Funakoshi,* Paul had heard other things. Sadistic killings. Murder without cause.

Paul sobered after his short meeting with Ahm Baqa. From then on, he searched every face in the crowd. His fear began to grow again.

One day, to his surprise, Ludwig began instructing him in celestial mechanics during lulls in the dart booth's activity. Paul felt his interest stirring, and brought some tapes to his cabin. He studied early into the morning, and learned quickly.

Between the morning meal and k'rati, there was a scant two hours of free time, and these Paul often spent with Shimmy, exploring Shad's central city or watching the ships in the spaceport. To tell the truth, there was not much to see on Shad—endless jungle, harvesting machines, and the few cities themselves. This one, the capital, was an amalgamation of slums and business districts, devoid of artistic or aesthetic interest. The inhabitants were friendly enough, but openly envious of what they perceived to be the opulent life-style of the circus. In the slums, Paul saw things which contradicted much of what he had previously thought of the Empire. Paul found on Shad a second reason to distrust the Emperor, and it disturbed him deeply.

On the fourth day, Paul and Shimmy were walking in a particularly blighted section of town. Ugly brick buildings burned in the sun, without a tree in sight to relieve the glare. Many of the houses were boarded up, their windows shattered, gaping like open mouths. They saw lounging people of all ages, grown torpid from the heat. The faces of the people were hopeless, frustrated, avaricious.

The scene depressed the boys profoundly, and they

began to retrace their steps, away from the smell and filth.

Someone bumped into Shimmy. He brushed around him, but the person back-pedaled and bumped into him again.

Paul and Shimmy looked into the faces of three youths, possibly five years older than themselves. There was a sneering look on them, as if they had just encountered something unbelievably uppity and disgusting.

Shimmy made as if to go around them again. The oldest one placed a hand on Shimmy's chest, and stood him there, dirty fist dangling.

Shimmy looked directly into his eyes. Paul could see his friend's skin turning red, to match his hair. When his voice came, it was soft and conciliatory, as if he were talking to his oldest friend.

"Hey," Shimmy said, "we're leaving." Gently, he pushed the arm away.

It came back again, harder. The Shad youth was smiling now, and the other two formed a loose semicircle around them, cutting off escape.

"You 'ave come onto the wrong side of the street, my dear," said the oldest of the three. "You see, this here is our side, and we don't like no strangers here." The voice was loud and drawn-out, as if for the benefit of unseen listeners. Paul glanced at the boarded-up windows around him. There was no one there.

"All right," said Shimmy, smiling. "We'll go to the other side, then. Come on, Asa." He took a step into the street, with Paul at his side.

Again the arm intervened. "First, you hotshot spaceman, I want to see the color of your money . . . you got money? I want to see it."

One of the other two was just in front of Paul. Paul watched him as, expertly, he spat onto Paul's shirt, just above the waist.

Redness came over Paul's vision. He barely heard Shimmy say: "This is a waste of time. Give him your money, Asa . . ."

Paul had only been in k'rati four days. But already he knew, or thought he knew, some of the most basic moves. He kicked upward in a snap kick, landing deep in the other's stomach. The other bent forward in an explosive grunt, and Paul changed feet and kicked him in the face.

Both Paul and his opponent fell violently backward.

He heard Shimmy say, "Oh, no!" in that same uncanny softness. Paul recovered and turned, and beheld a knife in the hand of the oldest youth, moving like the striking fangs of a snake. He yelled a warning. The third youth jumped at Shimmy, arms flung wide.

And suddenly, Shimmy was not there. The third attacker encountered an outthrust leg, and went sprawling. The older one felt his knife arm break, as it was caught between Shimmy's knee and chopping fist. He screamed.

And Shimmy and Paul were running, out of the ghetto toward their own end of town.

"Why are we running," Paul yelled, outraged. "We could have taken them easy. We could have finished off the other two."

Like a cobra, Shimmy's open palm struck across Paul's mouth. Tears of shock sprang into his eyes, and he stopped, openmouthed. Shimmy stopped and glared at him in a rage, and shook his fist in his face.

"Asa, you're the dimwittedest moron I ever did see," he yelled. "We could have gotten out of that without taking them on at all. Blast you! What's the point of slugging it out for no good reason?"

"They were stealing our money," Paul shouted, still outraged. "We don't need to take that from anybody!"

Shimmy nearly danced with exasperation.

"Why, you idiot, you've taken k'rati for four days, and you think you're a black belt and can beat up the whole Empire. You don't know a thing about it. The first thing that you must learn is that you don't need a temper, that it interferes with a clear head. And the second thing is to avoid a fight whenever you can. I would have given them my two marks, what difference does it make?"

They stood in the street yelling. People paused to look, then went on, not wanting to get involved in it.

"First they take your two marks, and then they take away your pride," Paul hollered. "I don't need it. If I'm going to stand up straight, I won't put up with any two-bit . . ."

"SHUT UP, will you, will you just shut up?" Shimmy paused, sweat pouring from him. He shook his head as if to clear it, and then looked at Paul again.

"Now look what's happened to me," he said quietly. "I've gone and lost my temper, which I haven't done for three years. You *are* the most frustrating bubbleheaded nitwit I've ever run across."

Paul glared at Shimmy defiantly. Shimmy threw up his hands, and turned to walk down the street. Paul followed.

"Look, P . . . Asa," Shimmy said. "I won't put my self respect on the line either, but you've got to weigh the actions with the consequences. In this case, we can weigh five marks against our own injury or death, against injuring or killing *them,* and against letting out the secret that we on the *Funakoshi* practice k'rati. Oh, Baqa would just love that!" He added, as an aside: "And if you hadn't gotten those lucky kicks in, maybe I couldn't have handled all three of them. Then what?"

There burst from Paul indignantly: "'Lucky kicks,' my eye. I knew just what I was doing!" He felt a glow of strength in him, radiating through him like the warmth of Shad's sun.

Shimmy waved his arms at that same sun. "Why me?" he asked it. "Why do these things always happen to me?" Then he turned to Paul.

"I said 'lucky kicks,' and I meant 'lucky kicks,'" he lectured. "No matter what you think, you don't know the first thing about k'rati yet. What do you think, four days and you're an expert? Your balance was all wrong. Your kick had no snap at all, just sheer muscle. You didn't have your hands up; if the other guy wasn't such a clod, he could have wrapped his fist around your ear."

Paul felt the warmth fading. His brow furrowed in concentration. His pride fought against it, but he remembered how he had fallen backward when he landed that second kick.

"You've got to understand that k'rati is something that you never really *know,*" Shimmy said. "It takes almost three months before you can really handle yourself on the street with it, and two years is better. Before the three months have passed, you're better off whaling like a windmill than trying k'rati . . . you'd just make a fool of yourself, and get beaten to a pulp besides."

Paul walked rapidly, as if to put Shimmy's words

behind him. But his ears heard, and his mind remembered.

"The most important thing," Shimmy went on, "is to remember *not to use your k'rati ever, unless in the last extremity.*"

Shimmy became silent, and they walked to the entrance of the fairgrounds, both lost in thoughts of their own. Then Shimmy said:

"You know, Asa, in the old days, if the k'rati master found out that one of his students was using it in the streets, he'd come after him, and the student would be lucky to even come near the class again. Now I'm not telling Ahm Baqa about what happened out there, and I got a feeling those punks won't either. But you've had a mighty close call, that's all I can say."

Shimmy walked into the fairgrounds. Paul gazed after him, and his mind yelled:

But I didn't ask for k'rati in the first place!

CHAPTER 14

Bora, Amphor, Cleon, Potts. Also Marsay, Caldor, Arivale, Remanus, Swolt. The gray planet Caravel. The ringed planet Rona Cay. Dripping skies and swollen oceans passed before Paul's fascinated gaze; deserts, jungles, multiple moons, double and triple suns. The kaleidoscope of the Three Hundred Suns passed before his eyes, as the circus ship passed among the planets of the Empire. He saw, and heard, and grew, and learned.

A year and a half. Paul had grown taller, and was inconceivably stronger. He wore a belt in k'rati that was green, and felt confidence awash in him like the tide of an endless sea. He studied astrophysics, computer design, molecular circuitry, light amplification and transmission, gravitational synthesis, linguistics, sociobiology, atomic theory, interspatial mechanics. His education became far more complete than it would have been in the government-controlled skools of Elsinore.

He became a navigator. He could handle the computers on the *Funakoshi*, could hurl the ship through that twisted, multidimensional door that was called "interspace." He could pilot the ship in real space, and land it in a space smaller than the average house.

In short, he learned from each one of the crew members of the *Funakoshi*, as they had done before him. For every crew member was a generalist, a Renaissance figure skilled at many things, and master of some.

He befriended the exotic animals that the circus housed, coming to know their quirks and their needs, their consummate, profound individuality. Of them all, only the griff remained remote. It glared at the world with implacable, unyielding hatred, and Paul shuddered as he pictured the impossibly alien, savage world from which it must have come.

Shimmy remained his friend. With Jonny, a slight thaw developed, so that they dealt with one another civilly, with caution somewhere in the background. And toward Ahm Baqa, he developed a sort of awe, while at the same time puzzled by certain contradictions he perceived in the man.

He also studied the tapes in his cabin, finally able, through the influence of the period of silence in the k'rati class, to make some sense from the strange metaphysics that he encountered there. He became aware of Taoist and Ch'an/Zen teachings, of Sufic and Vedantist thought, and of Talmudic and Quaker ethics. He became aware of religion itself, that forbidden commodity lost in centuries of suppression and intolerance.

As far as he could see, the members of the *Funakoshi* did not hold to a particular religion among the multiplicity of those that they studied. Rather, they distilled a certain mixture of outlooks on life along with ethics and esoterics, and came up with the unique brew that made the *Funakoshi* what it was. They worshiped nothing, finding strength and knowledge within themselves. Yet where that strength and knowledge originated they did not know, any more than they could trace the origin of each thought that passed through their minds.

They confronted the mystery of living and dying, and found that it remained a mystery. But they were strengthened through the very fact of their confrontation.

And Paul found out something else. The contempt that the crew demonstrated for the Guard and the Emperor was not merely an expression of random and capricious rebellion. It instead had deep roots that went beyond the ship itself. Paul discovered that the *Funakoshi* was not alone, that there were others among the thousands of traders and merchantmen and Explorers that plied the starship lanes who saw the Empire in the same light as did the circus ship.

There was a loose federation of malcontents, flitting throughout the Empire, with a casual but effective intelligence network. The word "rebel" was never heard; but they called themselves the "Bel," so the idea, foreshortened, was there. Against them, the Guard waged a relentless and bitter war.

At one time Paul would have been horrified by all this. It would have been treason. But then he learned of the

Calais; and he heard of the blue planet Eliyahu, and began to understand what had gone into the formation of Jonny.

The *Calais* was an Explorer, whose crew were Bel in the same way as was the *Funakoshi.* Baqa had heard about it on Rona Cay, and his face was ashen white as he told it to the crew, just before the class. Shimmy whispered that Baqa had had friends on the *Calais,* and some who were rumored to be more than friends.

One of the crew members of the *Calais* had done the most foolish thing possible. One night in Spaceport Elsinore, he had become drunk, a stupid thing for anyone, and absolutely insane for a Bel crewman in the capital city of the Empire. He was sitting next to a local, who kept coming up with the obligatory jingoist statements of a citizen loyal to the Emperor—about the necessity for sky-high taxes to "defend the Three Hundred Suns from possible alien invasion" and similar baloney. The crewman pointed out that no intelligent alien life had yet been found; that the human stock on the inhabited planets discovered so far seemed to derive from a common origin, buried in a past so distant that the memory of it was lost. The crewman suggested that the Emperor was using the taxes to support a military clique of the rich to contain the teeming multitudes of the Empire, to prevent dissent and to promote their own profit. He suggested that the Emperor was a despot of the sneakiest kind, pretending benevolence while doing everything to kill off independent thinking and personal freedom. He suggested that the first citizen who took a blaster to the Emperor would deserve a million marks, but that he and his fellow crew members were not greedy—they would do it for free.

The citizen was a news reporter, and he was recording everything the crewman said, secretly. He left the bar and went directly to the Guard.

"Where did the *Calais* get that moron?" moaned Ahm Baqa. "Not only was he a suicidal blabbermouth, but his ideas were not at all what most of us in the Bel think. Kill off the Emperor to what avail? There is an inexhaustible supply of 'Emperors' among the militarists. He did not understand, apparently, that other measures are needed here, the kind that are more subtle and effective."

The Guard jimmied the *Calais*'s on-board computer. When the *Calais* jumped into interspace, its coordinates looked right on the ship's readout screen. But inside, the numbers were changing randomly by the nanosecond. The ship jumped, and no one, including the crew of the *Calais* itself, would ever know what coordinates were used, and where they had gone.

Baqa waved vaguely above his head, and Paul glanced automatically upward, to contemplate the ceiling of the gymnasium.

"The galaxy and the Clouds have an uncounted number of stars. The *Calais* could be anywhere. Almost certainly they are somewhere in deep space, with no reference points that the computer would know. Too far from a star for their solar collectors to function. Their only hope would be to jump at random, and hope that they land in a region near an inhabitable planet."

His voice dropped to a whisper. "And the chances of that are so remote, that the crew must be thinking of themselves as dead already. Their nuclear power will last a long time, but there will be famine, and thirst, and madness, and death. Eventually it will be a ghost ship, drifting alone in a coldness and emptiness that surpasses the capacity of the human mind to understand."

His gaze turned inward, and he was no longer talking to the class before him. They watched him, shaken.

"Two hundred people," he said in a terrible, lifeless voice. "Two hundred good people."

It was on another day that Jonny had a particularly difficult time in the k'rati class. He was sparring with a yellow-belted woman of uncertain age, whom Baqa had snatched from the Guard on Arivale. The woman was unskilled, and launched a kick which carried her off balance, and that she could not pull back.

The very clumsiness of it was Jonny's undoing. The blond boy was used to disciplined k'rati movements, and the kick went around his guard and thudded against his side.

He seemed transfixed for a moment, as if caught in the web of some deep-seated and uncontrolled passion. Then with a high-pitched yell, he went for the woman.

Then he was on the floor, rolling in pain. Ahm Baqa stood over him, mustache flaring. His voice pounded at Jonny like a thousand battering rams.

"You *can control it,*" Baqa roared. "It comes from nowhere, and you can send it nowhere. It is a habit. *You can break it!*" This last was long drawn out, blasting into Jonny's brain, causing echoes from one side of his head to the other.

"It's his anger," Shimmy said to Paul in answer to a question, after the class was over. "Jonny is angry so deep that it sometimes seems to take him over. It's because he's from Eliyahu. So you can understand what makes him the way he is."

Paul commented that he had never heard of Eliyahu.

Shimmy was astounded, and expressed his disbelief in terms that cast scurrilous doubt upon Paul's sanity. Paul responded indignantly.

"Remember I'm from outside. What you know from the Bel, we in the Empire never knew at all. We never even knew that the Bel itself existed."

Shimmy allowed that this might be so, and thought for a long moment. He contemplated Paul silently, until Paul became impatient. Then he spoke:

"Maybe you should know," he said slowly. "Maybe it would keep you away from each other's throat, if you understand him some."

Shimmy collected his thoughts. He began matter-of-factly, and as he went along, his voice began to pick up momentum, as the images that he was raising inflamed his soul.

"Eliyahu was a blue planet of profound beauty, as if chance had placed there the single most perfect combination of azure sky and blue-green sea, and vegetation that massaged the eye and inspired the mind to poetry. Humankind had been there for thousands of years, as they have been found on most planets of the Three Hundred Suns. The people were reasonably happy, with nation-states that were mostly democracies or republics. Life was long and full, and no one thought that anything could change it, so deep-rooted were the planetwide values of kindness and brotherhood.

"Then an Explorer came. It scouted the planet, and reported to the Guard. The Guard mounted its usual expedition of conquest, and came to Eliyahu.

"Eliyahu had no resources that are not found in abundance elsewhere in the Empire. Even its vegetation, while beautiful to the eye, had little commercial potential.

"So the Guard decreed that Eliyahu would become a pleasure planet for the rich of the Empire, a garden planet of hotels and resorts. The citizens would be the servants. Of course the nation-states were dissolved.

"The citizens refused. The Guard chose one of the smaller nation-states called the Zeben Commonwealth as an example.

"One night in the dead of winter, with outside temperatures two dozen degrees below freezing, the Guard dropped twenty-five nuclear devices on Zeb. Its cities were destroyed. Its rural areas were cut off from energy that was needed for warmth. Those that did not perish in the holocaust, froze in their homes. By the time several days had passed, there were scarcely a thousand people left alive in Zeb, out of over twenty million.

"The people of Eliyahu saw the light, as it were. They capitulated. Today Eliyahu is a pleasure spot for three-hundred-odd planets, while its natives live in the poverty that servants always 'enjoy.' Its nations are dead, and its ideals are dying. It has seen the Empire as it is, and was shattered by what it saw."

Shimmy stopped, moodily. Paul's mind was horrified, numbed by the images that Shimmy had raised. How the truth had been concealed from him! How the skool had lied!

"What about Jonny?" Paul asked at length.

"Jonny," Shimmy said, "stowed away on a starship and was jailed on Boothbay II. He escaped and lost himself in the slums. Baqa found him there picking his pocket.

"You see, Asa," Shimmy said, looking at him. "Jonny is a Zeben."

CHAPTER 15

It was now three years since Paul had leaped through the Empty and run into the nightclub district of Elsinore. He had long since had his hand and footprints altered to fit the model of Asa Baqa, and had allowed the doctor to make the voice change permanent. There had been no more brain scanners at the various planets' spaceports, and it was obvious that the Empire had completely lost track of him.

He was still a green belt, though of a high rank. Ahm Baqa was slow to promote, waiting for perfection of movement before moving to more advanced forms of k'rati. Shimmy was a black belt; Jonny was approaching it. Jonny's form was at least as good as Shimmy's, but his emotions were not yet under control. Everyone on the ship knew, however, that he would get there one day.

Paul had come to the point that he lost track of his mind in k'rati. When facing an opponent, and even when doing the peculiar, violent k'rati dances called *kata,* he found that his mind had stopped functioning, and that his body somehow *knew,* with split-second certainty, what was demanded of it. His speed therefore became quicker than thought, so that he moved in a blur of grace and power. He could chin-up with one hand, and run for hours without any effort at all.

He could control his breath. He found that breathing was the key to perfection itself. Once he knew how to breathe—deep into the stomach, in a continuous, steady rhythm—his endurance grew to be phenomenal.

"Never give up!" Baqa chanted at them. "Nothing can stop you. If you break an arm, attack with the other arm. If both arms are broken, attack with the legs. If the legs are broken, crawl and bite, hit with the head. Only death can stop you now. Never give up! Never! Never!"

Paul had not used k'rati outside of class, since the incident on Shad. It was something special, this art that he learned, not to be squandered or diluted. Its purpose was not, after all, to create a perfect fighting machine, but to create a perfect man—and that was something else entirely.

The Bel were excited by some new development that their scientists had been working on, as a possible lever against the Guard. The *Funakoshi* had had a hand in it through a special ultraminiature circuit design; Paul himself had worked on it. But the project was being completed somewhere else, and Paul not only did not know where, he did not know what it was that the ultimate result of the project would be.

The circus was just cleaning up after a successful run on L. Redbone IV, a mining planet in the Brask region. The miners were enthusiastic about any diversion, and consequently the circus had been packed every night of its three-week stay.

The Big Top was already down and loaded. Paul supervised the loading of the animals, using the appropriate tranquilizers and seeing to it that they were placed into their proper crates. Jonny worked with him, and there was almost friendship between them.

At last they came to the griff. For the two-hundredth time Paul looked into the red, feral eyes, unearthly in their rage and hate. The strange, vaguely man-like body hurled itself at the bars of the cage, and the awful shark's jaws opened in that terrible scream of death and power.

Paul regarded it sadly. He pitied it, but he knew that on its home planet, it would have been no better off.

To hate was its nature, and it could not be tamed or contented. It was an aberration of nature, pure and simple. The circus had often thought of putting it to death out of kindness, suggesting that death would be preferable to such an existence. But some crew members had protested: how can we know what is going on inside that cat-like beast's mind (what there was of it)? Perhaps it is happy in its own way. No one could know.

So it remained, probably because of the crew's reluctance to kill another being, more than any other reason.

Paul and Jonny looked at it. Jonny held the tranquilizer rifle, an air gun that would shoot a cloud of gas into the beast's cage, putting it to rest so that they could shackle it to the wall. He steadied the gun, and aimed it at the staring, wrinkled-yellow face.

Then something happened.

"Paul," a voice said loudly behind him. A voice that was flat and cold. A voice that was . . . *unfamiliar!*

Paul froze, his back to the voice. Jonny looked at him out of the corner of his eye, then said clearly:

"Should I shoot him now, *Asa?*"

Paul said absently: "Yes, yes, shoot him now." But his whole being was concentrated upon that unseen voice.

A hand grabbed Paul by the shoulder and whirled him around. He found himself looking into the eyes of a rat-faced man about his own height, with greasy black hair and bulbous lips disfigured by a crooked leer. Behind him, Paul saw four other men, and from their carriage and demeanor, he guessed that they were plainclothes members of the Imperial Guard. But it was the rat-faced man that commanded his attention.

The Finder! It had to be him, the bloodhound that the Emperor had sent out nearly three years before.

There had been rumors of him here and there. He had turned up on planets that the *Funakoshi* had visited, but the Bel believed that he had been moving by instinct, by that incredible sixth sense that a true Finder has. They believed that he had not grasped the pattern, did not know that it was the *Funakoshi* that was drawing him.

He had seemed to have no time sense, no way of telling whether Paul had been on a particular planet two hours or two years before. Thus he could not pick the *Funakoshi* out of the hundreds of ships that passed through the space that he scouted. The Bel had decided that mathematics was against him, that only chance could lead him to Paul.

It must be my lucky day, Paul thought grimly. And all of it is bad.

He looked for the Executioner, who was said to be the Finder's companion on this quest for Paul Cartier. But the Emperor's killer was not there.

"I'm Asa Baqa," Paul said coldly. "What do you want? There's no 'Paul' here that I know of."

The rat-faced man laughed. He held Paul in a powerful grip, and Paul resisted the temptation to break his arm.

Jonny had turned and regarded the men. The tranquilizer gun dangled loosely at his side.

"You had me fooled," the Finder said, cackling grotesquely. Paul could smell something on his breath, a combination of liquor and nicotine and who knew what else.

"Yes, you had me fooled for a while, but Haman is never fooled for long, not for long. When I came to the L. Redbone system, I knew it right away. I knew you were *here*, somewhere. All I had to do was follow my nose, so to speak, yes indeed, and here you are. My nose always does the trick, ha ha ha. I've got you now, sonny boy. The nose, it is never wrong."

The man cackled shrilly, and yanked Paul by the arm. Out of the corner of his eye, he saw the muzzle of the tranquilizer gun rising idly toward them.

Then, all at once, one of the four behind the rat-faced man moved. A finger blaster leaped into his hand. Deliberately he shot Jonny at close range.

But the blaster was set low, and its flame seared Jonny's arm. The blond boy cried out in pain. The tranquilizer gun clattered to the ground.

Jonny's scream mingled with the unearthly cry of the griff behind them. The five men paled, and looked nervously at it.

"I must have nipped the beast too," the Guardsman said. "But I think the blond kid was going to do something with that gun."

The griff hurled itself at the bars of the cage, its claws tearing at the barrier with inhuman strength. A piece of the mesh snapped clean, but the rest held. The griff beat upon the bars in insane rage, screaming horribly at the seven beings before it.

Paul prepared to move. He felt the finger blaster, nestled securely against his left arm. He knew that this was it, that there was no way of talking this human leech out of the idea that he was Paul Cartier. He knew that the man had the certainty of intuitive knowledge. No matter what he was otherwise, he was obviously a Finder of the first rank.

Paul would break the Finder's arm and draw his blaster. He would cut down the four Guardsmen if he could. If not, it would end right here. The Emperor would finally have his way.

Something caused him to look up.

Across the fairway, Ahm Baqa stood silhouetted between two wagons. He was standing in a crouch, his two hands holding something in front of him, as if to steady it. It was pointing directly at them.

Jonny was on the ground, writhing silently in pain. The

five men had their backs to Ahm Baqa. The fairway was empty of people.

Paul snapped the Finder's wrist like a dry stick, and flung himself on top of Jonny. The Guardsmen whipped out their blasters, momentarily confused by the Finder's scream.

"Lie still," Paul screamed into Jonny's ear. "Don't move for your life!"

Over his head, the tiny beam of light lanced past. Ahm Baqa had a laser key, and he was shooting its beam directly into the lock of the cage door.

The door fell open, and full upon the five Emperor's men fell three hundred kilograms of raving hatred and terrible strength and fury.

With blasters on full they fired at it as it tore among them, rending with its razor-sharp feet and claws and teeth. They screamed and tried to run, and they scarcely moved a step before it was upon them.

In moments it was over. Paul glanced up, and was sickened by what he saw.

The five men were dead or dying, lying strewn about the fairgrounds as if a scythe had swept among them with a buzz saw on its blade.

The griff, terribly wounded by their blaster fire, bent over one of them, worrying the body like a cat worries a rat. In awful pain, it stood like an avenging devil, raining hate upon a Guardsman that was altogether beyond caring.

Then Ahm Baqa came up behind it and shot it to death.

The Guard on L. Redbone IV slapped the *Funakoshi* with a crippling fine, even though the evidence left for them suggested that the Guardsmen themselves had inadvertently blasted open the griff's door.

As to the mission of the five men, the Guard on L. Redbone IV did not know what it was. Baqa said off-handedly to Paul that the Emperor had no desire for the true purpose of the Autobeneficent Aptitude Test to become widely known. Nonetheless, the "accident" had happened at the circus fairgrounds, and it would not take long for the Emperor's advisers on Elsinore to put two and two together.

The *Funakoshi* was in deadly jeopardy. It lifted off of L. Redbone IV with the certain knowledge that the Imperial Guard would attack within a few hours' time.

CHAPTER 16

The *Funakoshi* hurled through space toward the jump-point, building up speed. Aboard an electric excitement flowed, as the crew members became aware of the crisis that was at hand. For the first time in Paul's memory, k'rati class was deferred to a later time. The crew did the tasks that were necessary for the running of the ship, or gathered in the cafeteria, watching the big screen that ran along one wall. The screen showed the ship's bridge, and the meeting that was taking place there.

There were four people on the bridge. The three commissioners were there, and "Asa Baqa."

It was the first time that Paul had seen Aliyah, the elder commissioner, now leaning back wearily in a deck chair, her face the color of chalk. She was very old, and very sick.

Ahm Baqa said to him: "You are here, Paul, because this whole thing concerns you, more than anyone else."

"Paul," he had said; no longer "Asa." But there was no need of it anymore, was there, Paul thought.

He glanced at the screen in the wall on his right, where the assemblage in the cafeteria seemed to be staring directly at him. He did not like the loss of anonymity. He felt like an insect under glass.

"Our usefulness to the Bel network is at an end," Sylva, the auburn-haired commissioner, said distinctly. "The *Funakoshi* will be hunted down within the week; if a jumper relay satellite passes through Redbonian space soon enough, maybe within the day. I see only one alternative, and that is Casa Nueva."

Paul heard an indistinct murmur, and realized that it came from the group in the cafeteria. With a start, the obvious occurred to him: that there was a two-way visiphone open, so that the assembly could not only see and hear them, but they could see and hear the assembly.

"I concur," said Aliyah, her voice weak and tremulous. "We must not risk this ship nor the scientists aboard; it is too important to the Bel."

The crowd murmured again, with obvious approval.

"Wait," a voice said. Paul recognized it as Sven. Paul saw him in the screen, stepping to the front of the group.

"We still have a chance to warn the others, get them all together on Casa Nueva. It's time for a concerted effort to rid the Empire of that monster on Elsinore!" The assembly cheered, more at the last few words than anything else. Paul sensed no real discord here; rather, the determination to find the best possible course among various alternatives.

Sylva spoke up: "We have already sent a microwave transmission to our agents on L. Redbone IV," she said. "That's all the warning our people need. If . . . and that's quite an 'if,' since I cannot see how the Guard can discover the Bel conspiracy merely by the disappearance of our ship . . . if there will be any repercussions to the remaining Bel because of us, we could not improve the situation by staying among the Three Hundred Suns. Word will get around fast enough."

Sven sat down.

Paul waited for another objection, but none came. Apparently there was a consensus to head for Casa Nueva—wherever that was.

"I've got something I need to say," Paul said slowly. "You people seem to be overlooking the obvious solution."

He cleared his throat, and then said carefully: "Because, you see, I'm the cause of all this. You can save your ship—and the Bel—by turning me over to the Guard."

He looked around at the faces of the crew, waiting for a sign from them.

What he saw was a mixture of disbelief, annoyance . . . and amusement.

"It is not the time for stupidity or martyrdom," Ahm Baqa said humorously. "We have you, and by thunder we are going to keep you. Anyway, how do you expect us to explain to the Guard that we altered your fingerprints, changed your voice and gave you a new name, all without suspecting that you were a fugitive? Tell us, Paul, how are we going to explain all that?"

The expression on Paul's face was so confused that the crowd in the cafeteria rippled visibly with laughter. Paul said in a choked voice:

"What you're saying is, whether or not you want me, you're darn sure stuck with me!" He glared at Ahm Baqa.

"Take it like that, you paranoid!" Shimmy yelled from the crowd. The group laughed again.

"You're a free citizen just like the rest of us," Ludwig bellowed. "We turn *no one* over to the Guard!"

Paul gave up. He looked helplessly at Ahm Baqa, who looked calmly back, his mustache quivering with a suppressed smile.

Then Paul heard Aliyah's weak, strained voice. "The time-choosing is behind us," she said. Paul shot a look at her, but saw no malice there. He smiled gravely, and was astonished to see her aged face break into a wan smile that was a jumble of creases and lines.

She coughed spasmodically, as if to erase the smile from her face.

"All right," Ahm Baqa snapped, turning away. "Casa Nueva . . . it is decided." He looked into a locational device, contemplating their distance to the jump-point.

Aliyah turned to the screen.

"You may not know," she said feebly. "You certainly do not know, in fact, that no one of us knows all the coordinates of Casa Nueva. Were one of us captured and drugged, the Guard could not get sufficient information to locate our base. Now, however, there is no reason why I shouldn't share with you the information I alone have." The effort left her weak, and she slipped backward in the chair.

"Come here," she motioned preemptorily to Paul. Paul stepped over to her, and looked into a pair of incredibly brilliant, hazel-green eyes.

"I will tell you my third of the coordinates from Redbone to Casa Nueva," she said. "You will remember them, and be proud that you helped carry the *Funakoshi* home. Perhaps then you will feel more like one of us."

Paul began to protest that he already felt at home, but she reached out and drew him close. He felt her aged whisper on his ear, like the touch of a feather.

She recited a complicated formula to him, which he memorized instantly.

There was no need to repeat it.

"Now," Aliyah said to Ahm Baqa, "return me to my cabin. You have no further need of me here."

Paul would have protested again, but was silenced by a look from Ahm Baqa. Dumbly he watched as a pair of crewmen came and wheeled her out.

"So Paul," said Sylva, "you're a commissioner for the moment. Once we get to Casa Nueva, of course, none of us will be ranked anymore. But for now, how does it feel?"

Paul could find no words to say. He let the formula flow in his mind, and guarded it against forgetfulness.

Then a voice broke his reverie. It came from the ship-to-ship-to-shore radio on the bridge, like a message from Doomsday.

"*FUNAKOSHI!*" it said. "THIS IS THE IMPERIAL CRUISER *EXCALIBUR*. STAND BY FOR BOARDING!"

With an oath, Sylva hurled herself at the controls, and threw a relay which opened up the screens on the bridge. In a twinkling, it was as if the walls, floor and ceiling had dropped away, leaving the grandeur of space glowing all around them. The controls floated as if in a black sea, and Baqa and Sylva moved about disembodied, like wraiths in a boundless night.

The in-ship visiphone was left open, and Baqa snapped two words: "Battle stations."

Below, Paul knew, the crew was scrambling to get to their posts, to pull into action the *Funakoshi*'s hidden defenses. If the *Excalibur* believed it to be a defenseless merchant ship, they were in for an unpleasant surprise.

Normally Paul's station was at the lifeboats, but Baqa reached out and held him on the bridge.

"You man the auxiliary computer," he said tersely. "Double-check Sylva's figures. Program in your part of the formula when I tell you."

Paul seized the auxiliary controls, his heart racing with excitement. Tensely he monitored the figures passing across Sylva's screen, matching with his own.

Below them, nearly occluded by the blazing light of L. Redbone, there was a glowing dot. Ahm Baqa manipulated the controls, and the dot swelled on the screen until it took on the unmistakable shape of a starship.

"No doubt about it," he said quietly. "One of the Empire's most advanced cruisers. There must have been a jumper relay passing through Redbonian space at the worst possible moment."

Paul knew that there was no luck to be found here. The incident on L. Redbone IV must have happened just before the entry of one of the jumpers, and the response from Elsinore had already come.

"Time to jump-point," Baqa rasped. He stood hunched over the console, comparing the cruiser's course with their own.

"Two hours," Sylva said. She groaned. Paul could see what it meant on his auxiliary: for more than fifteen minutes of that two hours, they would be within firing range of the *Excalibur*.

"I must have the formula now," Sylva said. "I have to work out every alternate jump-point possible, in case we're slowed down or crippled."

Without a pause, Ahm Baqa recited his third of the formula. Paul followed with his. She nodded briefly, and fed the information in.

So ended Paul's reign as commissioner of the starship *Funakoshi*.

An hour passed. Paul felt sweat creeping into his eyes, and wiped it away. The *Excalibur* was a bright spot on the unmagnified screen, brighter than any star except for Redbone itself. Paul's ears pounded from the messages that poured through the radio—threats, cajoles, and funniest of all, appeals to patriotism.

"Shimmy," Ahm Baqa yelled into the intercom. "Load Lifeboat I with explosives and release it," he said. Then he yelled into the radio: *"Excalibur,* this is *Funakoshi.* We cannot slow down, for we do not have enough power in reserve to make it back to L. Redbone IV. We *have* to jump. Pick us up in Greystokian space."

Baqa paused in the midst of this multiple barefaced lie. He took a deep breath.

"We know what you want," he said loudly. "We are putting Paul Cartier in a lifeboat and setting it adrift. We will impound ourselves on Greystoke, and await your attention."

Paul gasped at the use of his name. The *Funakoshi* trembled briefly, and the angular shape of the lifeboat momentarily blotted out the stars. Quickly it shrank to the rear, becoming a pinpoint of bright, reflected light.

"We do not dare to jump early," Sylva said. "Our entry into Casa Nueva is tricky at best, and an early entry would bring us too close to the system's sun."

Paul saw the analysis verified on his computer. Their hopes rested on the lifeboat, and on whether or not the *Excalibur* would slow down to pick it up.

"*FUNAKOSHI*, HEAVE TO!" the radio screamed. "WE WILL POWER YOU BACK TO REDBONE. IF YOU DO NOT DECELERATE AT ONCE, WE WILL DESTROY YOU!"

"The *Excalibur* is launching a missile of some kind," Ahm Baqa said suddenly. "But we are too far for it to reach us before we jump."

Several minutes later, a flaring explosion appeared soundlessly behind them.

"The lifeboat!" Paul breathed. "They didn't even stop to see if I was on it!"

"Aye," Ahm Baqa said. "There is the efficiency of the Guard." He looked grim. "They wanted you," he said, "and now they want us as well."

The dot that was the cruiser grew slowly behind them.

"Ten minutes to range," Sylva said after a time. "In ten minutes they will be near enough to fire on us, and I doubt if our defenses can stop them."

Ahm Baqa looked deep into his instruments, as if to draw from them an answer to the dilemma.

Finally he sighed.

"We have no choice," he said. "It will delay us, and there is always the chance that we will jump into something worse than this, such as a Guard patrol on maneuvers."

Paul was puzzled.

"Pick the most boring, least active, most peaceful Three Hundred Sun system for which we have coordinates," Baqa said to Sylva. "And one, of course, whose jump-point is available to us within the next ten minutes."

Paul slapped his forehead. Of course! What a halfwit I am, he thought. It would have been ridiculous to suppose that Casa Nueva's jump-point would be the first one encountered out here. With Three Hundred other known destinations, some of them were bound to fall earlier than the Casa Nueva coordinates.

"The earliest possibility is Perre. Fifteen seconds. Set coordinates 5789.3, 45789.2, 689000.0."

And no ship, Paul thought with a growing satisfaction, could follow another one as it jumped through that ill-understood region called interspace.

Baqa's fingers flew over the console. The *Funakoshi* jumped.

Thirty-three minutes later they flickered and vanished from Perrean space and angled toward an orbit around Casa Nueva. Of the *Excalibur* there was no further sign.

CHAPTER 17

It was a grim region of space, the junkyard remains of a dying solar system. The "sun" was little more than a glowing cinder, weakly casting a red glow upon the broken remains of its satellites. It was a system that an Imperial Explorer would glance over and reject in a minute—which was one of the reasons that the Bel had singled it out.

Even the nova that had wreaked such havoc on the system's planets had been weak. Casa Nueva itself was a rutted and jagged asteroid, relatively close in to the feeble sun. Perhaps once it had been part of a larger planet, but its atmosphere, if it ever held one, had been stripped away, and its elements fragmented, torn, vaporized and reformed, by the ancient explosion.

It was big enough so that the six-tenths normal gravity was tolerable, and round enough so that the horizon did not disappear like the edge of a cliff. But it was dark and forbidding, like a reddened ash of hell.

Obviously the Bel base was underground, to take advantage of the electronic and thermal insulation of hundreds of meters of heavy metal and rock. There were incredible expanses of natural and artificial caverns, tunnels and rooms, a warren of activity and life. It had been an engineering project of gigantic magnitude, and Paul's respect for the Bel organization increased immensely.

Once the *Funakoshi* had identified itself (and the identification had been confirmed), the base greeted it with open arms. The ship settled in a cylindrical hole at the base of a crater, which was promptly covered over by a manhole lid of rock and metal.

An entry tube snaked to the ship, and the crew spilled over one another into the base that they had never seen.

They were aliens returning to a mythical and legendary home. Those Bel ships which, like the *Funakoshi*, circulated through the Empire, had never dared to jump out of the regular traffic lanes—it would have been too easy for the Guards' computers to compare arrival and departure dates throughout the Three Hundred Suns, and discover the gap. People and intelligence were exchanged through carefully orchestrated jumps by a dozen Bel starships which had previously "disappeared" into deep space forever, as far as the Empire was concerned. The ships would jump into regular space to emerge almost side-by-side with Bel ships on routine jumps within the Empire. Then the transfers would proceed between the two, using lifeboats and microwave.

The transfers never took longer than an hour, after which the ship from Casa Nueva would veer away and jump again to the Bel base.

Only once had Paul himself witnessed this, when the *Funakoshi* transferred its molecular-circuit portion of the secret project to a Bel ship. It had taken weeks of preparation, involving intricate message-sending through Bel contacts throughout the Empire. No deviation occurred in the schedule that the Guard required the *Funakoshi* to post. Nothing unusual could have been suspected.

All the effort could have been avoided, of course, had the rebels known that the *Funakoshi* would itself soon "disappear." But it could not have been foreseen.

Paul entered eagerly into the life of the Bel base. He saw there the first Bel children that he had as yet seen, though he understood that there were some on other starships. The life was communal with plenty of opportunity for privacy. He found himself assigned with Jonny and Shimmy, continuing their technical and philosophical education with others who were more or less at the same level of study.

And there were the inevitable k'rati classes, with a huge following and many new techniques.

And he found out what the secret project was that he had heard about and worked on. There was no danger here of betraying the secret to the Guard, and everyone on the base knew. It was nothing less than the perfection and micro-miniaturization of the Matter Transmitter, the most effective weapon ever conceived by man.

The Empty!

Paul remembered the moment, so long ago, that he had hurled himself into the murky gray screen of the Empty on Elsinore, and passed from certain captivity into the anonymity of Spaceport.

At the time, influenced by the newscasts he had seen, he had felt that he was being miniaturized, reduced to a molecule and beamed across town. But now he found that it was not true.

The Empty did *not* shrink and then transmit like a radio wave—that had been a smokescreen invented by the Emperor to conceal the true principles from the conspiracy that he vaguely sensed around him. Rather, the Empty involved a distortion of space, in somewhat the same way that the starships employed when jumping through interspace. It created a situation where, in effect, the two screens were a single plane of space and time, so that someone entering one of them would perforce come through the other, exactly like passing through a doorway.

That transmission was restricted to line-of-sight was a myth; the Empire had simply not yet learned to manipulate interspace from two different points over a long distance. It was conceivable that once this problem was overcome, the need for starships could disappear, except for exploration.

Paul could see it in his mind's eye. Perhaps some day, to go from one star system to another, all one would have to do would be to walk through an Empty screen.

And there was still something else to think about. For when the Empty was perfected, the Emperor would have a powerful weapon for economic blackmail, to hold over his own supporters' heads. If he could destroy so easily their economic base, their entire way of life, he would then have the power to become an Emperor in the furthest sense of the word, an absolute tyrant, without even the slight restraint which the rich now forced upon him.

It was this, the Bel believed, that the Emperor planned, and they were working feverishly to beat him to the draw, to perfect the Empty first.

Paul had been there for six months when a special meeting was called. He gathered with the two thousand or so others who inhabited Casa Nueva, in a vast cavern that functioned as an assembly hall. There, he sat with Jonny and Shimmy, and looked down upon a platform where the elected commissioners sat. Of the dozen or so, one was Ahm Baqa.

A hush fell over the assembly as the oldest commissioner, an aged gray-haired man, stood to address them. The Bel sat riveted to their seats, as the old man's voice rolled out of loudspeakers toward them.

"As you know," he began, "the Emperor has long suspected that there was some kind of movement against him. But thus far he has always looked to the rich industrialists for the source, and has not suspected that the movement could have arisen among the educated, poorer segments of his society.

"But the *Funakoshi* incident has apparently made some sort of impression on him. His perceptions are evidently changing, and the change harbors no good for us."

The commissioner cleared his throat. No other sound broke the ominous silence in the great hall.

"Today," he went on, "we have received word that the Guard has begun a crackdown on the independent ships ranging through the Empire. The Guard has instituted a computer-based system of the identification of ship personnel, to identify their movements, their background, their skills. Within two months, no one will be able to join a Bel ship without being detected, and the Guard will be able to perceive the scientific expertise that our ships have built up over the years.

"The Emperor will certainly be able to put it all together, merely by coordinating the knowledge of the ships and crews that he receives. But that is not the worst of it.

"We understand that the Guard has begun a systematic campaign to squeeze what information they can from selected navigators, and eventually from all of the skilled personnel aboard our starships. They will use mind drugs, truth serums, brain scanners, torture—whatever they can. Within perhaps a month they will be able to identify the Bel conspiracy, and should have enough information to identify the coordinates for Casa Nueva itself."

The rebels looked at one another, aghast. This was a disaster of inconceivable magnitude, with a potential for the utter destruction of the Bel society. A ripple ran through the crowd, and swelled into a babble of outrage.

The commissioner waited for the tumult to die down. He waited for a long time. Gradually the crowd became aware of his waiting, of the quiet presence that he radiated like a cold torch. They quieted, and waited for his next words.

"Thus," he said at last, "the commission has decided to call in all of our starships remaining in the Empire, to call in what agents we can, and to erase all knowledge of the Bel, insofar as possible, from the Empire."

The import of his words sank into the assembled Bel. They glanced with new dismay at one another.

The commissioner went on: "As of a week from today, we will be isolated completely from the Empire. We will have no intelligence, no ships, no agents functioning in the Three Hundred Suns. We will be cut off absolutely from mankind, and have no way of knowing what the Empire is doing, or whether or not they know of Casa Nueva."

He was silent again, for a moment. The crowd did not speak. They sat as if benumbed, as if waiting for the last blow to fall.

"We await discussion from you," the commissioner said at last. "If there are any alternatives that we have not explored, please bring them up now. The last crisis is upon us; our fate is before you now."

Nobody stirred. It was as if it was a ballroom of statues, sitting immobilized in a silent and eternal assembly. Horror moved through the crowd, and despair. But no overt display arose, as the crowd waited for the last words to come.

"We must prepare," the commissioner intoned, "for the arrival of several thousand refugees. But more importantly, we must finish the project as soon as possible. We must be able to reenter the Three Hundred Suns within a year, or it will be too late. Unless we perfect the Empty, which the Emperor will surely do within that year, we will become a lost colony out here on Casa Nueva, cut off from the Empire, with nowhere else to go."

He turned and sat down. The crowd filed out in an eerie silence, scarcely broken by the sobbing of children being hushed by their parents.

CHAPTER 18

It was a homecoming of immense proportions. For a time, ships fell like rain, until the space surrounding Casa Nueva was dotted with nearly eight hundred gleaming cylinders in staggered, multitiered orbits.

All efforts of concealment were abandoned. There was nowhere on Casa Nueva that eight hundred ships could hide. The commissioners discussed sending unneeded ships into deep space; but every circuit and steel plate was necessary to the effort ahead.

There were two schools of thought. One feared that the Guard might already have put together the three sets of coordinates needed to discover Casa Nueva. They urged abandoning Casa Nueva, and setting out to find another base, before the Guard had a chance to attack.

The other school argued that the time this process would take was not available; they were so close, so very close, to mastering the Matter Transmitter. Any delay could cause the Emperor's winning of the Empty race, and take the edge forever away from the Bel.

Naturally the Bel knew who had the coordinates, and who did not. So they knew, as the ships came in, how many chances remained for the Guard to gather together all three sets, or even one set for one jump-point. Each day the chances narrowed.

They heard of the suicides of captured navigators, who died rather than reveal a single coordinate.

The Commission decided to stay.

The base was a tumult of overcrowding, frenzied activity, reunions and new acquaintances. The corridors swirled with squalling children, cartloads of supplies, hurrying scientists, rumbling earth movers and equipment of every description.

Paul scarcely saw any of it. He was part of a team of microcircuit specialists, working tirelessly to synthesize the components which the theoreticians called for. When, after eighteen hours of frantic work, his eyes burning from peering at microscope screens, watching the patterns of molecular activity as he manipulated them . . . he walked then through the crowded corridors unseeing, his mind speeding as if stimulated by caffeine, turning over and over the possible solutions to the next set of problems which were confronting him.

They labored unceasingly for four weeks, their numbers augmented by the scientists from the ships that came in. The theoretical demands were, one by one, accommodated, and the equipment was, piece by piece, delivered. The last component was designed and fabricated. The last electrical pathway was etched in a wafer so thin that it would fall through the spaces between the molecules of the hardest steel. The last circuit was fitted into place, and a pall of silence fell over the scientists and technicians as they waited, gathering their strength, to see if it all worked.

It was a Cube. Paul gazed at it in a kind of horror, six faces of incomprehensible nullness, six sides of nothing. It floated in the center of the auditorium where the multitudes were crammed, supported by a single rod of steel that pierced a place where the emptiness was not. It was a weapon against which no shield could stand, and no force destroy. It was the Empty gone mad, turned from an intriguing method of transportation into a terrible instrument of annihilation.

"It is a logical development of the Empty screen," the old commissioner said matter-of-factly, his white hair eddying in the currents of air that entered the Empty screens and did not come out. "It is merely a six-sided Empty screen, with no access to the inside, other than what we ourselves devise.

"If it were not for that slight breach in one of the facets of the screen, where we inserted the steel support," he said, turning toward the grayness, "it would shoot away, cutting through anything in its path. It would retain the momentum, but not the gravitational influence, of the planetary and solar systemic spin. While the planet went on with customary ellipse, the Cube would take a straight line, a tangent out of the system.

"But you must understand that it is exerting no force against the rod, trying to escape. It is utterly inert. It is unaffected by gravity, air currents, light, heat, impacts of any kind, magnetism, electrical forces, radiation . . . anything.

"It is, of course, opaque from the inside since nothing, including light, can enter it; and it's opaque from the outside due to the space-twisting ripple effect of the Empty field itself. Anything already inside a Cube can pass right through to the outside, but nothing can enter a Cube from the outside without being transferred to the companion screens.

"However, it *is* possible to get into a Cube's 'insides.' There is another, smaller Empty screen inside the Cube, by which we can reach into the mechanism from our own screen in the laboratory. We have cables running into it from there, and we can lower any part of the screen, like this . . ." and he pushed a button on his wrist, where-upon the foremost facet disappeared, and the crowd could see the mechanism inside, still radiating the five other sides of the Cube . . . "or we can drop a small piece of it, such as where the support rod holds this work-ing model in place."

He touched the same button, and the sixth side snapped on again. He went on:

"We can maneuver it by placing jets or rocket pods in-side. As you now know, anything can *leave* the Empty screen from the inside. A rocket mechanism can push the internal parts of the Cube from the inside, and carry the Cube itself along with it. But if that same rocket were to try to push the Cube from the outside, it would simply pass through the Empty and out wherever the companion screen is located.

"The companion to our model Cube is, by the way, several kilometers away. The effect is as if this Cube and the companion Cube were one, with no physical space in between. The companion matches this Cube in every respect, even to the hole where the rod goes in. Passage from the Cube to its companion is, as far as we can determine, instantaneous; the distance between them is in some way erased.

"I'll show you some of the potentials of this weapon." The commissioner took a steel crowbar and waved it at an edge of the Cube. The end that touched the edge of the Cube was gone. He held up the gleaming half of the bar that was left.

"Anything that intersects an edge of a Cube will be sliced at the plane of intersection, and nothing can prevent it. In this case, half of this crowbar is now in a chamber, several kilometers from here."

He paused to let the import sink in.

It took a moment for Paul's mind to comprehend the meaning of what he had just seen performed. But then his mind grasped the enormity of it.

If a Cube were hurled at a ship and did not swallow it completely, its edge would cut through the ship like butter. There was no question of shooting down a Cube, as one would shoot down a missile. In other words, unless a ship could avoid the Cube entirely, it would be doomed!

And if the Cube were large enough to engulf a whole ship, that ship would reappear wherever the companion screen was located. If the companion were elsewhere in space, far from the "battle" entirely, the ship would appear there, effectively silenced.

But what if they were to place the companion screen in a lethal location, such as in the bowels of a planet . . . ?

"We can hook the Cube into another Cube as its companion," the commissioner said, "or we can provide for several interrelated Cubes, and switch companions from one to the other as need be.

"For example," he said, still regarding the gray emptiness of the Cube with sober, even somber intensity, "what if we sent one Cube deep into the heart of a sun? By placing the companion in deep space, the resulting gout of solar energy would dissipate harmlessly. But if we switched the companion to a Cube which was close to an enemy ship, that ship would be vaporized instantly by the explosion of plasma and energy which would pour out of the Cube. We could switch this fearful weapon off and on at will."

Not a sound came from the vast assembly. It was as if they were dumbstruck in the face of supreme power, afraid of the responsibility that was suddenly theirs.

"We can shield our ships completely with Empty screens, and yet still maneuver through space," the commissioner continued. "Not only our Cubes, but our ships as well, would be indestructible. Our molecular engineers have designed the Empty so well that a foot soldier could have a screen, even a Cube, of his or her own.

"The only real danger we could face, would be for the enemy to discover our home base and attack it. Yet that obstacle is simply overcome, too. For all we have to do is enshroud the base in a Cube, and nothing could win against it. Anyway, each ship will soon be a 'home base' in its own right, once properly equipped.

"Can we cover an entire planet, or even a solar system, in a Cube?"

The commissioner smiled. "Not yet, but of course eventually we will—it is simply a question of power and size. Picture, if you will, two interstellar powers possessing the Cube on a planet-sized scale. Each would be unconquerable. And to answer an obvious question, you cannot attack a Cube with another Cube. They simply do not accept one another—they slide apart like greased rubber balls. In fact," and here the commissioner allowed himself another smile, "someday we may use intersecting Cubes in lubricated joints. Who knows?"

The crowd began to stir. Everyone's thoughts were rushing to complete the picture that the commissioner had presented. The necessities of the situation were becoming obvious, as the pictures of the puzzle fell into place.

"We must abandon Casa Nueva, of course," the commissioner said calmly. "We must climb again into our eight hundred ships, and cover them with Empty screens. At the first possible moment we must invade the Empire, and seize the reigns of power before the Guard perfects the Empty.

"If the Empire were an alien power, such an action would be immoral and repugnant. But they are our people, our species, held in bondage and deceived by money- and power-hungry men. If they are a part of the species' destiny, we are a part as well.

"We cannot stop the Guard altogether, of course," the commissioner said. "Even if we had the numbers to completely conquer the Empire, eventually refugees of the old order, somewhere, would perfect the Empty and embark upon a ruinous civil war.

"All we can do is this, if we would rejoin the human race. We must tell the people of the Empty, and keep it from being the province of a small group alone. Even in our hands, it could become the instrument of the worst dictatorship that humankind has ever known. But if every planet of the Three Hundred Suns had it . . . then no one planet could control the other. With each planet indestructible the only alternative would be harmony and cooperation.

"We would go beyond balance of power to balance of safety. Every planet would be absolutely safe from the other.

"Chaos? Yes, at first. And what if each locality had an Empty? Or each human being? The chaos then can scarcely be imagined. But it would end, it would end. When it's a choice of cooperation or impotence, the human being will always choose cooperation, interaction with his own kind.

"Some of you may say that we are playing gods here, taking hold of history in a way that no small group should. But it is either that, or letting the Emperor's group take hold of it instead. With the Empty Cube, they can hold the human race in benevolent bondage forever. And they will, unless we seize history for our moment, and open up humankind to potentials that the Empire could not and would not provide.

"Perhaps it is a cruel choice, but we must do it. We must do it. We have no rational alternative."

CHAPTER 19

Fifty ships broke into Elsinorian space; the remainder scattered among the Three Hundred Suns. Casa Nueva was abandoned. The Bel put all of its resources in a final, fateful push.

Paul stood on the bridge of the *Funakoshi*, and saw his home planet grow larger on the three-hundred-and-sixty-degree screen. Ahm Baqa and Sylva stood with him, Baqa's hand resting on his shoulder. The Guard was out there, and they all knew it.

They ran down toward Elsinore, and to the casual eye, nothing would have seemed unusual about each Bel ship's appearance. The casual eye was not likely to notice the tiny satellites that accompanied each ship, nor to guess that these could become the deadly weapon known as the Cube. Nor could they guess at the impregnable shielding which each ship carried. The Empties were switched off, held in reserve as a surprise to throw the Guard off balance.

The Bel plan was simple and bold. To each planet of the Empire, they were already beaming a media-wide message that described the Empty and what it could really do. They described their intent: to establish no-cost Empty stations on each planet, through which access to any planet of the Empire might be instantly effected. They described their intention of reintegrating themselves into the Empire. They suggested that any Guard interference with the phenomenally simple and cheap transportation which they offered, would be an unconscionable interference with the citizens' basic rights. They suggested that it was all a question of the greatest freedom for the greatest number.

And on most of the planets, they knew, the ships would overcome minimal Guard resistance, land, and set up the Empty stations, and demonstrate them directly. The Bel figured that once the citizenry saw what Matter Transmission could do, woe would befall any Guardsman who interfered.

The Guard would be telling another story, of course. They would call the Bel advance the alien invasion that they had always postulated as an excuse for more and more weaponry, more and more military control. They would deny everything that the Bel said, including the Empty capabilities.

But they would not have much time, for the Empty

potential would soon become evident through the Empty stations, and especially through their own defeat.

But it was on Elsinore that the Bel expected the most bitter resistance. For here the Emperor was held in near god-like status, and here he would be expected to concentrate his strongest defenses against the "alien" invasion.

The fifty Bel ships approached Elsinore in a loose V formation, broadcasting their message with a power that overwhelmed all but the closest channels of communication.

Yet they were still a hundred million kilometers out, when they encountered the first Guard resistance.

To the Guard ship, it must have seemed strange indeed. They launched their most powerful missile at the "alien" invaders. They watched it arc through space. They saw it approach the rebel ship.

Then they saw confusion. It was as if their eyesight were blurred by an instantaneous grayness around the rebel ship.

It happened in an eyeblink. But the horrifying thing was that all at once the missile was gone.

They dismissed it as an illusion. They launched more missiles. The missiles disappeared in flashes of grayness. The Guard exploded missiles in space, to bathe the area in radiation. The rebel ships blinked gray as they passed through the area, with no apparent harm.

The Guard directed a laser at the leading Bel ship. The laser beam entered a patch of grayness, and disappeared. No sign of the laser beam was left.

Panicky, the Guard launched a flurry of missiles and beams, and turned tail to flee to Elsinore. They did not notice the tiny satellites that whipped past their ships.

A Guard ship met a Cube. It loomed in front of them. Possibly, they knew what it was. They had all seen the experimental Empties on Elsinore.

Frantically they tried to avoid it. It held its position dead ahead of them, rockets flaring out of its uncanny grayness.

And it was on top of them. They entered the blank gray wall, and space around them altered. They found themselves outside a Cube in a region of space that they had never seen.

The companion Cube receded rapidly behind them, and they could not track it. It was as if they were trying to track nothing.

They became lost in a nameless region of space.

"I hope the blasted fools do not go jumping about all over the universe," Ahm Baqa said, watching the Imperial ship disappear into the Cube. "If they pay attention to the homing beacon that we put out there with the Cube, they can hang around until we come after them. The beacon is so far from the Cube that they will never relocate the Cube itself, and will not be able to reenter Elsinorian space. They have gone on a one-way journey, and I hope that they realize that their only recourse is to obey our instructions. If they jump into interspace, they will be lost as surely as was the *Calais*."

More Guard ships appeared, and for a while, Paul was lost in the split-second activity of a space battle.

A Guard ship embarked on a deliberate collision course with a Bel cruiser. For a moment, the two ships seemed to melt into one another, but it was an illusion only. When it was over, the Bel ship was there, and the Guard ship was not.

The only weakness which the invaders had was that when all Empty screens were on around the ship, it was blinded. A cable snaked through an Empty screen inside of the ship, through a companion screen in a satellite which hovered over the ship for just this purpose. A screened ship saw a scene from a point of view somewhat apart from the ship itself, and this confusion often caused a particular navigator to delay lowering his or her screens until sure of absolute safety. The tendency was for an inordinate number of Bel ships to be screened, and partially blind.

It was this factor that caused the *Damariscotta* to lower its screens in the face of a Guard laser attack, something that could not have been predicted only moments before. When the helmsman realized that ruby destruction was lancing at the speed of light toward him, he was already dead. The beam bore directly down the *Damariscotta*'s vertical axis, cutting a doughnut hole completely through the ship. A few persons survived behind airtight bulkheads that were untouched by the beam. Most of the crew died.

"Beam the wreckage through an Empty screen to the rescue area," Baqa yelled to the closest Bel ship. A sort of first-aid station circled in far orbit, for just such an eventuality.

The *Damariscotta* would go down in history in what would be described as the Great Battle of Elsinore. For it was the only Bel ship that was damaged in any way.

Four thousand eighty-one Guard ships attacked the Bel that day. For a time, the forty-nine remaining invaders were utterly surrounded, peppered by missiles and lasers from all sides. Through it all weaved the awesome, frightful Cubes, which swallowed ships like gigantic vacuum cleaners, sweeping the Guard from the Elsinorian sky.

When it was over, four thousand and three Guard ships had disappeared through Cubes, as if they had never been. Seventy-eight Guard ships had outsped the Cubes and fled to Elsinore, where they were later overcome on the ground.

Fifteen hours after their entry into the Elsinorian star system, the rebels held sway in the space surrounding the home planet of the Empire.

But they were sobered by what they found there. Outside of the capital, the populace was panicking, disbelieving the rebel broadcasts.

And the capital itself was shrouded in the grayness of an Empty screen.

If the Guard had not perfected the Empty, evidently the Emperor had. And he was hidden now behind an impenetrable screen, working on who knew what plots to destroy the Bel.

CHAPTER 20

Paul and some twenty-nine others stood in a loose circle around the Empty half-cube that concealed the capital from the eye and from all possible avenues of invasion.

All possible avenues, that is, save one.

The rebels knew, because of the nature of the Empty screen, that there was possible entry somewhere underground. Somewhere the capital was connected to the rest of the planet, perhaps in a column of bedrock, perhaps in a hundred little pockets, perhaps everywhere. For if it were not attached to the planet, the city would have shot off in a tangent as the planet curved away along its orbital path. Gravity, after all, has no effect on an Empty.

Somewhere, under the city, there were surely holes in

the Empty defenses. The Emperor could scarcely suspect that the Bel technology had advanced so far, as to enable individual screens and thus individual access to those holes.

For individual access they had. Paul held the equipment on his back, in a knapsack so light that he scarcely felt it. There were twenty-nine others like it, all that the Bel had had time to manufacture. The strike force stood at equidistant points around the city, waiting for the signal to move.

They knew that the Emperor was not stupid, that he may have prepared for underground invasion. They knew that they would have to rely on their wits, and their k'rati speed, and their luck. They would have to go in and turn off the city's screens, and capture, if possible, the Emperor himself.

The signal came. Jonny, Shimmy, Paul, and twenty-seven others extended their right arms and pressed a button on their wrists. Out of sight of one another in a ring around the city, as one man they began to move.

Paul enclosed himself in a partial Cube, top, sides, and front. Not the bottom—for then he would have fallen straight down in the direction of the planet's core. The rear screen was only a partial one, from ground level to a third of the way up, to keep debris from cascading like a rockslide against him.

Protruding from the pack was a tiny airjet, pointed downward. It was fed by an Empty screen the size of a quarter-mark. Paul could use it both for breathable air, and in an emergency as a source of locomotion. Should he have to, for example, he could tuck his legs under him and, with the jet full on, shoot like a rocket up or forward, his screens effortlessly slicing through whatever obstacles found themselves in his path. But balance and directional control would be a problem, and Paul intended to avoid that method of travel if at all possible.

So Paul pointed the partial Cube downward, toward the city. He began to walk.

The Cube sliced into the ground as if it were air. He built his own road into the bowels of the planet. The pavement that he had been standing on vanished in an instant, to be replaced by hard-packed clay. Then gravel. Then the bedrock itself.

An occasional verbal report issued from his headset as the orbiting Bel monitored his progress and that of the twenty-nine others. The Bel wanted to give the Emperor's technicians as little chance as possible of detecting their transmissions and interfering with them, so the reports were taciturn in the extreme, no more than a welcome touch with the outside. By the gravitational disturbances caused by their passage through solid rock, the Bel were able to pinpoint their locations under the city and transmit the information to them through the planet's crust on ultralow frequencies. Without this information, of course, they would have been completely blind, with no idea where they were headed or what lay above them. There was no other way for them to "see" through solid rock.

At one point the headset informed Paul and the others that one of the thirty had blundered into an underground river and, by rocketing forward, only barely escaped being drowned. Another found the rock beneath her feet disappear into a spectacular underground chasm and, in her mad scramble to both avoid a fall and control the air-jet "rocket," had found herself many meters off course.

In general, however, Paul had little idea as to the exact location of the others. He had to leave it to the orbiting Bel to coordinate their attack from above, to whatever extent they decided was best.

At length Paul was told that his long walk through the almost featureless stone was nearing its end. The Emperor's palace lay above him. Grimly as he climbed upward Paul thought about what might face him above. The Guard would be there in force, he knew, and they would hurl at him everything that they held in their arsenal.

When he was centimeters from the surface Paul stopped and methodically went over his plan of attack. The problem was to use the Cube just enough to shield him from the Guard attacks, while at the same time gaining enough visibility and mobility to reach the throne room and the Emperor himself.

Paul knew that he would have to be shielded on all four sides and on the top, and leave himself only enough room on the bottom to walk forward, and to keep himself attached to the gravitational pull of Elsinore. But such an arrangement presented two major problems, when considering the action of the Cube.

For one thing, the Cube was opaque from both inside and out. How, then, would he be able to see?

The other thing was even more of a problem. Even if he were able to see, he would have to keep his forward screen lowered into the floor, to stop blaster energy from seeping under it. Rather deeply into the floor, in fact, or the blaster could simply blow the floor beneath him away. But what would happen then as he stepped forward?

The forward Empty screen would do its job, and transmit any matter that it encountered.

But of necessity, it would encounter the floor. It would cut away a part of the floor in front of him as he moved, to the depth that he set the screen. When he took another step, he would be stepping into the recess that his screen had just cut. And meanwhile, his forward screen would cut still deeper into the floor in front of him.

Paul had a ridiculous vision of himself tumbling into the subbasement as a result. If he weren't already in the subbasement . . .

To counter these two problems, the Bel had been able to think up only crude solutions, in the short time which they had had.

To counter the vision problem, they had devised a thick piece of lead-imbedded, thermal glass. Paul called for it now, and as he drew his forward screen back toward him, the glass was thrust through the companion screen in orbit above him and clattered into the space between the screen and the rock. He turned off the screen, went forward and picked up the glass, and stepping back turned the screen on again.

The glass's coupling fitted awkardly up on his left arm, braced against his body by a rigid triangular fitting. It was heavy and inconvenient. The weight dragged on his arm. It was a short term solution, and it would not be long before he would have to have a period of rest, or discard the contrivance altogether.

Since the glass was coupled with the arm that projected the Empty screens, he could make a space in his forward screen, and it would move in harmony with his arm. Thus any vertical or sideways motion of the screen would not slice the glass off—the glass would move with it.

The solution to the slicing away of the floor was rather more satisfactory. Because of the sophistication of his molecular circuitry, Paul was able to oscillate the lower part of his forward screen, so that it bit into the floor and back up again, many times a second. That would be no good against the concentrated, steady energy of prolonged blaster fire—enough energy would leak through to fry Paul to a cinder. So a second Empty screen was placed there, perhaps five centimeters behind the first. The second screen was only a half-meter high, so that it would not interfere with the glass plate. But more importantly, it was hooked into a phase exactly opposite that of the first Empty screen. When the first screen oscillated down, this one went up. When the first went up, this one went down. Again, many times a second.

The circuits were designed so that the frequency of the oscillations of the screens was determined by the rapidity of Paul's forward progress. Thus the only damage to the floor would be a series of hairline slices, which Paul would scarcely notice. The floor would not be cut away from beneath him. And no blaster or other energy or matter could come through the first screen without hitting the second.

The design was excellent, Paul thought with satisfaction.

It was time.

Paul lowered his screens around him, keeping the forward screen somewhat in front of the glass plate. The plate would have to wait until he emerged into the open. Down here, it would merely run into the rock he was walking through and stop his progress dead.

He angled steeply upward, and climbed, watching the floor carefully.

The rock gave way to gravel; the gravel, to a thin layer of plastic and tar; then reinforced concrete.

Then his feet passed over ultra-tile, and he was no longer climbing.

He had emerged.

Now he eased his forward screen backward, until it reached the six centimeter-thick glass. Carefully, he fitted the screen around it, making a hole in the screen, as it were, through which passed the glass. He made certain that there was not the slightest gap between the glass and the screen, through which a deadly burst of energy might pass.

He looked out at the inside of the palace for the first time. It was remarkably like looking through a tunnel one-third meter square.

If only he could have used television circuitry, instead of this thrice-confounded glass! But nothing electronic would have been able to stand up to blaster or laser fire. Thermal glass, on the other hand—heat-resistant glass able to darken instantly at onslaughts of energy, thus protecting his eyes, and clear again when the energy passed —thermal glass was just the return to basics that the situation seemed to demand.

A fancy, cubicle "pair" of sunglasses, he thought incredulously. Sunglasses!

He was in a corridor. On his forehead his headlamp had been switched off, and a television circuit turned on which fed information to the Bel base.

Paul waited for the technicians to figure out his exact location within the palace, to tell him in which direction to proceed.

The corridor was white steel-plastic, the prevailing building material of the Empire. It was by no means featureless, however. Niches held busts of the Emperor. Doorways opened up to who knew where. Mobile paintings shimmered in translucency and kaleidoscopic color.

From a doorway, a little way down, someone strode out. The man turned and walked hurriedly toward Paul. He wore the clothes of a technician or Imperial adviser. His face was haggard, his manner preoccupied. How he was helping the Emperor to meet this crisis, Paul could not even guess.

Paul watched him, a half-smile forming on his lips. The man was looking directly at him, walking directly toward him, and did not see him. Or rather, saw him and didn't notice him. Too many thoughts were crowding through the man's mind.

What did he see when the picture in front of him finally coalesced in his consciousness?

A gray mass, nearly filling the corridor. A gray nothing with a square glass eye.

The man's mouth opened in a shout which Paul could not hear. The man turned, with the obvious purpose of fleeing headlong down the corridor. Fear lent power to his legs.

Paul sighed. Doubtless the Guard knew that he was in the palace somewhere, and would find him in short order. Taking this underling out would not solve that problem.

But whatever this man's role, it could not hurt to take him out of the game, and perhaps put a small hole in the people who formed the Emperor's defenses.

The man was just reaching momentum when Paul stopped the oscillation of his forward screen and caused it to leap forward, closing the hole for the glass, and then leap back again. In an instant the screen was around the glass and oscillating on the bottom again, protecting Paul from attack.

But from Paul to where the man had been, there was a thin slice taken out of the floor. And the man was gone.

Paul's thoughts were interrupted by the soulless voice which came from his headset.

"You are of course on the lowest level of the palace. Above you, perhaps six floors, is a wide corridor which leads to the central throne room. As you know, no one outside the palace knows what exactly is inside that room. We can only infer that its defenses are formidable."

All at once, something happened outside Paul's Cube, carrying his attention away from the voice. All at once, the corridor changed into a seething inferno of radioactive fire.

Paul saw where it came from, an instant before his glass opaqued and cut off his vision. It came from everywhere. Rather, it came from points at five centimeter intervals, about midway up the corridor's walls.

It was a spray of blaster fire, lethally mixed with radioactivity. It engulfed the corridor and everything in it, for as far as Paul had been able to see.

The Guard had detected him. He wondered if anyone had been in the corridor behind him. He wondered how many of their own people the Guard had killed.

In a single motion he turned the airjet on full, tucked his legs under and partially closed the screen beneath him. He roared upward, angled slightly forward to avoid impacting the glass upon the walls and ceiling that the upper screen was slicing through. A blast of heat hit from below, but it was too short to have any effect. In a trice he was two floors up, and the glass cleared.

A corridor flashed into view. A startled company of Guard, who had been walking away from him, looked around.

The fourth level found him half in a corridor, half in a room as he struggled to maintain a straight trajectory. Through the glass he saw the insides of a computer, and realized that his screens had sliced it half away, ruining it utterly. In the corridor a woman halted openmouthed, her right foot thrust out rigidly in a step, centimeters from his screen.

She drew her foot back and saved it. She was lucky. He wondered if he were swallowing up anyone as he rose. Or worse, slicing half into someone behind him, where he could not see.

He came through a room on the fifth level, with no view of the corridor at all. A water pipe which he had sliced through showered his glass with wetness, cutting off his vision.

Someone cut loose with a blaster, and his glass

opaqued. When it cleared, the sixth level was dropping to meet him; the blaster had burned the wetness away.

For an instant he took the consummate risk that this mode of travel demanded, turned off his front and bottom screens, and angling himself onto the firmness of the floor, turned the airjet off.

The room was empty, and Paul scarcely paused to inspect it. He turned toward where he knew the corridor lay, pushed out his forward screen without the glass, and walked blindly forward until the texture of the floor told him that he had reached his goal. Then he drew the screen back around the glass and peered through it. He turned in the direction in which he knew the throne room to be.

Twelve meters in front of him, he saw a platoon of Guardsmen. The hair on the back of his neck prickled, and a tremor ran through him.

He saw that they had a mobile blaster, motorized on wheels. Within seconds they had deployed it—a machine with enough power to vaporize his glass within three seconds.

Barely conscious of it, Paul's mind fell away. The necessities of the tiniest instant of time caused his thinking process to stop utterly. Here it was that Ahm Baqa's training became the instrument of Paul's self-preservation. Someone who has not k'ratika, would have died.

Convulsively, Paul's arm seemed to wince. His forward screen leaped out and the screen engulfed the Guardsmen, engulfed their machine. In another instant, the screen was back with him, surrounding the glass. And the corridor ahead of him was empty.

No, not empty, not quite. There was something on the

floor up ahead, something which twitched. Paul went closer. His eyes picked it out. Nausea arose within him.

A human arm, wrapped around the trigger of the vanished blaster. Paul had not had time to close the "window" which housed the glass. The slicing effect of the edge of the screen had done its grim and ugly work.

Paul sent the arm through to the other side of his forward screen. The Bel doctors would take it and graft it back onto the Guardsman. The Guardsman would become whole again, with only the memory of pain.

Again, the impersonal voice came over his headset.

"You are fifty-four meters from the doorway to the throne room. It lies directly ahead of you, neither above nor below."

Paul adjusted his forward screen for fifty-four meters. He closed up the "window" as he shot the screen forward. He also let the side screens travel along with it. And he turned off the little oscillating screen in front of him.

His forward screen engulfed everything and everybody in its path. His side screens closed the corridor off utterly to anyone in the rooms on either side.

He flicked his headlamp on. He faced a featureless gray corridor, with only the floor to relieve the gray monotony.

As he walked, he allowed the side screens to shorten behind him, in step with him. He was like a collapsing rectangular telescope.

With knowledge of the armless Guardsman's eventual recovery, his mind was clear. But there were thoughts—it was not a Yogan blank.

For he knew that he was approaching the final crisis. Now he would, one way or another, meet the Emperor. Either the dissolution of the Empire itself, or a resolution of its crisis, was before him.

He did not see how the Emperor could win; yet wasn't the Emperor supposedly the "luckiest" individual in all the Empire?

But was Paul's presence a sign that the ruler's luck was wearing thin, in the face of Paul's own proven fortune? Or would the Emperor's luck hold out, to the ruination of the Bel?

This matter of luck—it had been with him for nearly four years, and he did not understand it even yet. As far as he could see, he had had to sweat and work and study and strive along with all the rest of them. In k'rati he had felt pain and had been beaten. He had brought crisis to the Bel, rather than good fortune, though how it was to end was not yet clear.

Luck did not follow a rationally chosen path. Once again Paul considered the greatest puzzle of all. Who determined the path that luck would follow? Who determined what was "lucky"? Riches were not. Painlessness was obviously not. What was the supreme pinnacle of luck, anyway?

Was it power? The Emperor had it, all right. But Paul did not, except in his own self-confidence, his own inner strength.

Or maybe luck carried each individual into unguessed realms.

But what happened when one supreme luck ran into another? How could either prevail? Yet what if one person's goals were irrevocably opposed to another's? What then?

How could one supremely lucky person defeat another who was also supremely lucky?

Was it luck, or trained reflex, that had enabled Paul to engulf those Guardsmen who had been on the brink of blasting Paul away?

All he had was questions, Paul thought as his gray corridor shrank to a box. Questions, and no answers. The answers lay only a few meters beyond him, in a room which he had never seen, in the form of a person that he had once revered and now despised.

He braced himself, for the crisis was upon him.

He fitted his forward screen around the glass, and gazed into the throne room.

CHAPTER 21

It was big. Perhaps he had seen a bigger room before, he did not know. Perhaps the claustrophobic surroundings of three years of starship living had changed his sense of proportion. Again, he did not know. What he did know was that it was big, so large that the other side was lost in a dimness of haze, behind the dais.

The room was a gigantic half-sphere. It was smooth, without features. It arced from where he stood, geometrically to a high center, and down again.

Rather than white steel-plastic, it looked like steel itself —a strange, archaic self-indulgence on the part of the Emperor. It did not shine. It gleamed dully, like a poorly polished mirror.

Strangest of all were the globes. Four of them, spaced evenly around the upper regions of the dome. Not touching each other, and as far as he could see, not touching the dome itself. What held them there, he did not know. They were monumental, huge. He would have been awed by their size, in any other room but this.

The globes were steel, like the dome. They would have formed a floating square, if lines were drawn from their centers. The center of the square was directly below the center of the dome, a configuration of perfect circular and angular symmetry.

And directly below the centers of the dome and the imaginary square, there was the dais.

Why did he think of it as a dais, Paul asked himself. Yet he could not get the word "throne" out of his mind.

But it was more an obelisk than a dais. A round, extremely elongated cone, nearly a cylinder. It rose out of the steel floor in the exact center of it, and towered into the air.

It reached halfway up, and then changed. A minaret-like, droplet-shaped bubble of glass replaced it, sitting on top like ice cream on a cone and glistening as if it had just been polished. It was alight with internal illumination.

And in that glass near-sphere there sat a man.

For the first time, Paul saw the Emperor.

Paul strode deeper into the room. His forward screens cut tiny etchings in the floor as he moved. His glass weighed upon his arm.

He was still too far away to see much detail. The man was tall, but not unusually so. Gray-haired, with power virtually erupting from his demeanor, his very form. Self-assurance on a scale that Paul had only seen in the most intense of k'rati classes.

The ruler was sitting in a chair, studded with buttons on its ornate arms. The two men looked at each other, across a gulf of moral adversity and age.

Paul moved closer, alert for the slightest hostile movement. While there were doubtless many doors arrayed around the semisphere, none of them opened. No Guardsmen came in, no ray attacked. The floor was smooth and even, with no electrical rods or other tricks. The radiation detector remained quiet.

Paul could hear nothing. No sound had come through his screens, of course, and the glass was too thick. But his ears strained nonetheless, waiting for any sign of hostility.

He held the glass nearly to his nose now, the forward screen around it, to provide the widest view. His steps were short to the point of tiptoeing, to avoid sending his foot through the forward screens.

The obelisk loomed up as he approached it, the Emperor's figure taking on a progressively greater and greater grandeur and power. His awe was tempered by his knowledge of this man's nature, of his savagery and cold cruelty.

Paul paused, over halfway to the obelisk. Action seemed to be indicated, but he hesitated. He could slice the obelisk off at its base, of course. Or he could send the Emperor through his forward screen, into the hands of the Bel. But he hesitated.

And then the Emperor moved his left arm over a button on his throne, and pointed with his right. Paul's eyes automatically followed the direction of the imperial hand, and decision was taken away from him.

For one of the four globes had become transparent. And inside it, he saw something that he had not seen for over three years, and had nearly despaired of ever seeing again.

In that globe, on a platform inside it, surrounded by starkly staring openings of portable blasters, was his family.

His mother, and father, and brother and sisters. All of them were there. Obviously they could not see him, for they sat huddled in a tiny group. Paul saw the kindness of his mother's face, etched with more lines of care than he had seen on it before. His father's eyes burned with dull anger, as he looked around methodically for escape.

The Emperor's left hand hovered over a button on his throne. There was no mistaking his message.

Another hostile move, he seemed to say, and your family will be alive no more.

Paul's mind reeled in a paroxysm of frustrated, helpless agony. Fear was there, and hate. Both stood in him like companions, like old friends. He raised his arm up toward the Emperor, and moved his finger to send him to the Bel.

The Emperor's finger hovered closer to the button, touching it. The cruel black eyes grew dull.

Paul hesitated. Could he do it, before that finger moved? Could he?

His mind swayed. He could not be sure. What if he risked it, put his family's life on the chance that his own hand was quicker than the Emperor's? And what if he lost?

The idea could not be borne. It was a risk that he could not take.

And in that moment of realization, Paul knew that he was beaten. He knew that he had lost. Whatever level his luck could take, the Emperor's luck was greater.

The Emperor raised his left elbow, to show how easily the weight of his arm could fall on the button below it. The imperial mouth curved in a grimace that was both smile and leer.

Again, the message was not to be ignored. Paul's time was up. Either give up now, or watch them die.

Paul raised his arms and yelled at the heavens that he could not see. With a convulsive movement, he turned off his screens.

He pulled himself out of his backpack and sent it clattering to the floor. He stood erect before the Emperor. His arm felt light, relieved of the glass. He rubbed it, and looked into the face that mocked him above.

The voice came from nowhere, as it must have done many times to the retainers and sycophants that frequented the throne room.

"Luck," it said, that hated word, floating on the fetid air of the throne room. "You were the only one of the invading scum who made it through. Therefore you must be very lucky, and hence you could only be Paul Cartier."

"A brilliant deduction," Paul said bitterly. "Particularly in view of *their presence*." He pointed at the transparent globe, where his family sat immobile.

"You were the only one who *could* have made it," the voice said matter-of-factly. "So naturally I took precautions, to stop you by any means at hand.

"But enough of this," the Emperor said, waving his right arm carelessly, foppishly. "I will kill you now, at my leisure, and you cannot resist. But first the finger blaster, if you please."

Paul gasped. How had the Emperor known?

Six Guardsmen came around from behind the obelisk. Paul wondered if there was an elevator that opened there from below.

No matter. Reluctantly he disengaged the familiar weight of the tiny blaster on his left forearm. He sent it clattering at the feet of the Guardsmen who were in front of him.

Then they moved forward, armed of course with military blasters, some of which were out and pointed at him. But one of the Guard was big, muscles rippling through his skin-tight uniform, a black band on his arm.

Paul recognized him at once. It was the Executioner.

Paul faced him, his body instinctively drawing itself into a defensive stance.

The move was not lost on the big man before him. The Executioner threw his head back and laughed.

"Kill him," the Emperor said coldly.

The big man nodded, and came forward, drawing a double-edged knife out of his belt. A knife with which he was so expert, that men said he could draw and stab with such swiftness that the victim never saw the blade.

Paul knew that death was before him, and he had no time to prepare. But every living thing, he thought, is prepared for it. It is inevitable and natural. You do it without effort, with no way to stop it. It was built in, something that could not be escaped.

So Paul faced it phlegmatically, without fear. He would resist it to the end, but he did not fear it in itself.

The black armband came suddenly forward. The blur

that was the blade was not a blur to Paul's k'rati-trained eyes. His left hand swatted the knife hand aside. His right arm dove at the man's stomach.

The man leaped lightly back, plainly surprised.

The Emperor watched, fascinated. He could have had Paul killed instantly by blaster fire. But he preferred, apparently, a slowness to it, something that he could watch and, in some twisted way, enjoy.

The Executioner feinted with his other hand, and drove in with the knife. And Paul did something which he was required to do, in a moment that needed the most intense effort and power. It was an integral part of k'rati training, the basis of breathing, the wellspring of endurance and strength.

Put your hand over your stomach muscles and tighten them. See how tight they are. Now open your mouth and yell from your stomach, use it to force the air out through a reluctant throat. Feel those same muscles as you yell. They become incomparably tighter. They become as a rock. And the power flows from them, into the entire body. It is ready for anything.

Paul yelled that terrible k'rati yell, as his body drove forward. He kicked the knife out of the Executioner's hand, and drove the same foot into the man's stomach with a snap like a whip.

The stomach was stone hard, from years of physical training. But the suddenness of the attack, and particularly the yell, had unnerved the Executioner. He had never faced any real resistance. He had never met a k'ratika before.

He stumbled backward, and Paul moved into him in a

flurry of punches and kicks. And he made his hands into tools which were deadly weapons.

He stiffened his right hand, palm spread flat and fingers arced into a hook. His arm shot out, and the palm clapped with stunning force over the killer's left ear. The eardrum burst like paper. The man screamed.

The hand whipped back. The whole movement was a single, blurred curve. The hooked fingers tore the earlobe off as they came away.

The hand no sooner reached Paul's body than he sent it out again, this time with fingers outspread, slightly curved inward at the joints so that they would not break backward. They went for the eyes.

The killer, maddened by pain, was still a formidable force. His arm arced upward in a nearly perfect, but unlearned k'rati block. Paul's hand was batted away.

But the hand came back, this time with the fingers hooked again. But they turned flat, in a driving movement from the waist, the classic k'rati punch turned into something deadlier. The bent finger joints were a blade of rigid strength. The man had no time to bring his arm downward and bat the hand away.

The blade drove into the Executioner's throat, and he went down. He clutched his throat, gurgling. His eyes popped outward.

Paul yelled up at the angry figure on the dais.

"Your man is dying; his windpipe is crushed. If you want to save him, he must be worked on right now!"

"Let him die," the cold voice said. It sent chills through Paul's mind.

"Kill him," the voice commanded again. But this time

it was directed to the five other Guardsmen, the ones who held the blasters.

Paul, unarmed, could not hope to resist them. Their blasters came up, pointed at him, while their leader choked on the floor.

At that moment, Paul saw a gray something come into the room, on its far side.

His heart leaped. Another invader was there.

Whoever it was could think with the rapidity of light.

"Look!" Paul screamed. The Guardsmen hesitated, looking back to where Paul's eyes were obviously staring.

The invader's *upper* screen lanced out. It went far up into the room. It came under the transparent globe which housed Paul's family. It expanded, became wide. It danced up and swallowed the globe.

The imperial voice shrieked. The Guardsmen turned their blasters on the invader's glass eye, and blinded it momentarily. Whoever it was, could not see to attack.

But the Guard forgot about Paul. A side thrust kick broke a Guardsman's back. His yell was drowned out in blaster noise, as Paul's fist crashed into another's skull. The other three began to turn toward him, but to Paul's manic, adrenalin-powered metabolism, they turned in slow motion, like cartoon characters on a screen.

A blaster flew high into the air as its holder's arm was violently broken. Paul kicked the feet out from under a second, who sprawled ungainly, his weapon clattering across the floor. The third man's blaster was almost in Paul's face as he drove his knee into the Guardsman's stomach. It went off, singeing his hair.

But the man was down, and out.

Hurriedly Paul grabbed his backpack and directed a

screen at the Guardsmen on the floor, sending them to the Bel and to medical help. It was something he could not expect the Emperor to do.

Paul looked up. The Emperor was rigid, his left hand pushing a button as if to send it through the throne. The face was contorted, whether from fear or hate or both, Paul could not tell.

He donned his backpack, and hesitated.

And then, again, decision was taken away.

From an end of the room some distance from the newest invader, a door opened and a man walked in. He held a rifle blaster. He also wore a peculiar lump on his back, like the hump of a hunchback, or . . .

"Jonny!" Paul yelled. "Don't do it!"

Jonny lifted the rifle, and pointed it at the obelisk, at the bubble on top.

"Emperor!" he yelled in a controlled voice of savage power. A voice in which hatred and anger were absent. A voice of determined courage.

"This is for Eliyahu!" he yelled, his voice like a whip of doom. His blond hair shimmered in the light of the blaster fire that he hurled from his weapon.

The fire erupted through the air and engulfed the glass bubble. The bubble melted away like butter, exposing the figure within. Fire roared through the figure like light through a wraith, burning the throne into a rubble of twisted wires and burning plastic.

The smoke cleared. Jonny stood there, his blaster still, looking at the top of the obelisk where the throne had been.

Paul gaped. The unrealness of it sapped his mind. He

too stared at the top of the obelisk, not believing what he saw.

For the Emperor was there, untouched. He sat as he had on the throne, but the throne was gone. He sat on nothing, suspended as if by magic, hanging in the air. A sardonic smile played over his lips.

Paul's vision went double. He shook his head to clear it. Across the room, the second invader had snapped his screens off, and was walking forward. It was Shimmy.

Jonny too was coming forward. Paul saw dazed disbelief on the two faces, as they looked at the Emperor.

"It's a holograph," Shimmy croaked. "He's not even there. It's an image, a projection. He's somewhere else!"

"Aye," Jonny said, his voice steely. "But where?"

Paul's vision went double again. He reeled backward, keeping upright with difficulty. A terrible headache seemed to be coming over him.

"Hey, something's wrong with Paul," Shimmy shouted. The red-haired youth began to run forward. Then, inexplicably, he stumbled and nearly fell.

Paul looked into the sardonic face above him. He looked at the rigid left hand, still pressing a button that was now gone. He saw four hands, then, pressing four invisible buttons. He shook his head, and his vision would not clear.

He opened his mouth. Jonny seemed stupefied, the steeliness gone. Shimmy had slowed to a walk, picking his way carefully as if walking on eggs, though there was nothing there.

"Nerve gas," Paul gasped. "It must be nerve gas. He's gassing us, and we're standing here taking it."

He fumbled with the controls to his screens. He couldn't seem to make his arms work. The glass fell onto the steel floor and clattered away. His vision blurred until nothing was clear anymore.

The sardonic face above him was smiling broadly, as if party to a monumental joke.

Paul tripped. His vision cleared for a moment, and he saw two Cubes in front of him, glass eyes staring blindly outward.

If they were rational, they would send me through to the Bel, Paul thought vaguely. But the gas has got to them too, and they can't think straight. I've been in it longer, and I'm dying. If this room were not so large, I'd be dead already.

He forced his hand onto the controls. He chuckled as an amusing thought went through his head, but forgot what it was.

He punched at his controls. The two side screens winked on. Then the rear screen.

The face loomed over him like a mask of death. He blotted it out with the upper screen. He tried to punch the forward screen's button, and could not do it. He tried again, and his finger slipped nervelessly off. He raised it like a dead weight, and pressed it down.

His thoughts grew more confused, as the gas cut off more impulses to his brain. His hand slipped from the forward button, and fell over the button that controlled the bottom screen. The forward screen, he noticed, was on.

The bottom screen snapped on. Paul looked blearily around him, trying to focus his eyes. His air jet roared, forcing clean air into his Cube. Still, he could see nothing clearly. All around there was grayness.

Then a thought occurred to him that sent a shock of fear through his body. It cleared his mind more than anything else could have done.

No wonder he couldn't see anything. All six of his screens were on!

What was going on outside? He was now a Cube, with no opening at all.

The thing that he had most feared had happened. He must, at this moment, be a projectile shooting away at a tangent to Elsinore's orbit. Because gravitational forces could not reach him. He was completely encased in a Cube.

His fumbling hands found the controls again, but again they missed their mark. They snapped all the screens off at once.

He looked around at a crazy pattern of blue and gray. He was above the city, above the flat screen that protected it from the Bel. He must have torn right up through the throne room's roof, through the top of the palace, and through the screens that covered the city. Now he was spinning crazily like an emptying balloon, as the air jet roared uncontrolled.

His body would not function. When he saw the city's screen coming toward him, he somehow encased himself in all six screens again. Maybe he had reached the city's screen, he did not know. If he had, he must have bounced off it like a basketball.

When he turned the screens off again, he was high over the countryside outside the city, which was receding into the distance.

Paul's mind knew that he was in deadly danger, but he could not get his body to work properly. The air jet was somehow turned off. He was falling toward the ground, and his hands would not come together to reach the controls.

The trees rose up to meet his hurtling figure. He got his lower screen turned on, but it did not stop his downward plunge. It cut into the ground, but his body was veering sharply at an angle. The side of the hole that he was digging came up to meet his head. He ducked, and presented his back to it. It rammed into him like a mountain.

Pain was instantly followed by blackness. His tortured mind slipped away.

CHAPTER 22

The Emperor's face on the life-size screen did not seem at all unusual. It was the same face that Paul had once revered and now despised. It held the same expression of forthright candor and clear-eyed integrity. Even from his "bed," where he could feel nothing, Paul felt revulsion.

The announcer's scraping introduction was long over. The Emperor had begun speaking to his people. More than ninety-nine percent of the population of the Three Hundred Suns were tuned in. They tuned in to know how the Emperor had met the crisis of invasion—and defeated it.

Ahm Baqa, Shimmy, Jonny, Sylva, Vera, Sven, Ludwig, all were grouped around Paul's "bed." They watched the Emperor's performance breathlessly, but their expressions held something else as well. Paul decided that it was pleasure—a humorous kind of satisfaction.

For they all knew exactly what the Emperor was going to say.

"And the invaders proved," the imperial voice said, "to be misguided members of the human family. I say misguided, but not evil. No, not evil at all, for they brought to us the blazing human achievement that is the perfected Empty screen.

"I would not have chosen to have had it revealed in quite that way," he said deprecatingly, with a little half-smile. "Their way was unnecessarily violent. They had worked up in their minds all manner of misconceptions about your—and I will say our—government, and that is unfortunate, but hardly disastrous. For when I brought them to see things as they really are, they repented. Yes, I say, repented. They came to see that mankind was whole and strong and free after all.

"I do not blame them. And you should find forgiveness in your hearts, as I have in mine. Weigh their recklessness against the benefits of Matter Transmission, and see them as prophets in a wrong time. See them as wanderers brought to the straight path."

Doubtless the people sighed. With relief that the crisis was past; with full hearts at the generosity and benevolence of their ruler.

But the Bel arrayed around Paul did not sigh. They chuckled; they snickered; they guffawed; they laughed.

For the "Emperor" was a computer construct, a group

of Bel-created electronic impulses. His image was a fake. The Emperor himself was no longer there.

"I have stepped through one of the new Matter Transmitters, one of the new Empties," the "Emperor" said straightforwardly. "And I can tell you that it is not only safe, it is a joy to use. At last I can step from the palace grounds to any one of the Three Hundred Suns at a moment's notice. Never will any citizen of the Three Hundred Suns feel remote from me again."

"But after a time," Vera said softly, "the electronic image will convert to Wholeism and, feeling the religion in conflict with his imperial duties, resign. The transition to a planetary federation will be gradual and careful. The ordinary citizen will scarcely notice it, at least until he or she feels the new freedom."

The "Emperor" droned on.

"This I don't understand," Paul said, puzzled. "If that's an electronic construct, where is the Emperor now?"

The others looked at Ahm Baqa uneasily. Baqa said:

"Paul, do you recall anything after the nerve gas hit?"

"Not much," Paul said slowly, recollecting. "I remember noticing the Cube, though. And then the sky all around me. And falling." He shuddered, and pain shot through him. Confound it, he thought to himself. I must remember to keep still. It *hurts*.

"It's that blasted luck of yours," Shimmy began, a half-smile on his lips.

"Phooey," Paul interrupted him. "You made it to the throne room yourself. If you hadn't dropped my people through your screen at just the right moment, we would have been stopped right there. And that reminds me of something.

"Tell me, Shimmy," he said abruptly, "have you ever taken the Autobeneficent Aptitude Test?"

The question caught the red-haired man flatfooted. His face turned nearly as bright as his hair.

"Well, I . . . er . . . that is, I don't quite remember," he said incoherently.

"What he means to say," Baqa broke in, as Shimmy glared at him, "is that he scored almost as high as you can get. Why else did he come to the Bel? Indeed, have you ever asked yourself, how did we choose the thirty people in the invading party?"

"The aptitude test?" Paul asked, wide-eyed. "You mean that *all* of them had a perfect score, like me?" The thought was too incredible to be true.

"Not perfect," Baqa said, "but even so, why not? In the billions of people that inhabit the Three Hundred Suns, do you not think that statistically there would be others that would drop out, as you did? Why else would the Emperor have the test in the first place?"

Paul pondered that, and found nothing wrong with it. But the idea that his Bel friends were like him, luck-wise, was one that he had never considered before.

"But you must admit, Baqa," Ludwig said, "that it was nothing but luck that sent Paul's Cube in exactly the right trajectory to intercept . . ."

"By no means," Sylva cut in calmly. "If Paul hadn't done it, someone else would have. I knew we had the Emperor where we wanted when Shimmy destroyed the mechanism that controlled the city's screens. Of course it was only later that I learned that Paul had delivered the Emperor to us already."

"*I* delivered him," Paul stammered. He looked around the room. It was suddenly silent.

Then he looked at Ahm Baqa, whose dark eyes seemed lost in a great distance, with the palpable sense that many things had no answer, even when someone could name the question.

"Baqa," Paul said slowly, deliberately. *"What happened to the Emperor?"*

At last Baqa turned his eyes upon Paul, and they were sad somehow.

"This memory will stay with you and never leave," he began quietly. "But you must recall at all times that there is a destiny that no one can fully grasp until, perhaps, just after death itself."

He paused a moment, collecting the words.

"When you formed a Cube and shot off toward the ceiling of the throne room," he said softly, "you sliced right through one of the steel globes lying in your path.

"The Emperor was in that globe. His body was sent through your screens to the companion screens under the control of the Bel." He paused again.

"But I don't understand," Paul said. "What's the big deal? So we have him in custody; to me it looks like a lucky break."

"Oh, lucky it is probably," Baqa said slowly. "Certainly it is completely beyond our control.

"But I have phrased it poorly. You see, Paul, your screens did not take up the whole of the globe, nor did they take in all of its contents."

His kind voice went on, and Paul knew it all at last.

"The Emperor's body was sent through, along with most of his destructive equipment.

"But his head remained behind."

They asked after his family. Paul wrenched his thoughts away from the image that Baqa's words had brought to mind. He knew that he would keep returning to it, though, until time blurred the details and eased the horror.

But he recalled now the relief that he had felt, to learn that Shimmy had been fast enough, and that his family had fallen through to the Bel safe and sound. And when they had visited him in the sickroom, swathed as he was in the liquid splints and supports of modern medicine, their faces had shown their grief for him; but his had shown only joy, a joy which came to them, too, when they learned that he would recover and could be with them once again.

After a while another thing occurred to him.

"Listen, Baqa," Paul said carefully, not working his shattered ribs beyond their limit. "You cannot seriously believe that total luck is a force that would send me out of control into the countryside, to fall into a pit made by my own Empty screen, to hit the ground with enough force to break every bone in my body, and then to be buried by the rubble falling from the hole I made? That's luck??!"

"On the other hand," Baqa said, "there was the fact that you had turned partly over as you fell, so that your screen did not cut a hole for you to the core of the planet.

There is also the fact that torn up as it was, the mechanism of the screen still functioned, and we were able to come through it with a screen of our own, and send you through to the doctors. Where, I might add, we found that, given time and modern medicine and careful nutrition, you will make a complete recovery."

"But I'll be so out of shape," Paul said in such a miserable tone that they all laughed.

"Well," Sven growled, "our job's over now, and we're exiles again. We've instructed the Guard through the 'Emperor' to describe the Bel as 'deluded, but nice' to our fellow citizens. But they still won't like us much. It'll be mighty warm for us wherever we go."

"Aye, if we stay in their company," Ahm Baqa said.

Paul started. He was about to ask what Baqa meant when Sylva cut in.

"But you all know," she said unnecessarily, "that it was the only way. There would have been chaos if we had simply deposed the Emperor and taken over. There's one thing that human beings don't like, and that's to have one put over on them. They would have used the Empty screen which we gave them to invade *us,* and reinstate the Emperor.

"No," she said, "this was the only way. This way, it will seem to them that right has triumphed in the end. Most of them never knew the evil that resided in Elsinore, because his reign was outwardly benevolent. Only those that crossed him, came to know what he really was."

"Aye, it will seem that things are returning to normal again," Ahm Baqa said. "Whereas in fact there will be Bel behind the transition at all times. We will supervise, at least some of us, the coming of humanity into the age of the Empty screen."

"Some of us?" Paul asked at last.

"Aye," Baqa said, but again he was cut off, this time by Vera.

"And what about Jonny?" she said.

The directness of this query brought a blush to the blond-haired face. Ahm Baqa looked at him with emotionless, expressionless eyes. Jonny met the gaze, with a clearly visible effort of will.

"Ah yes, Jonny. There is another problem." Baqa turned and faced the group. "I might as well advise judgment now. Of course, it will have to be taken before the Commission, but I have no doubt that they will see it this way." He turned to the blond-haired man.

"You, whom we know as Jonny, have acted in a manner that was superficially contrary to the unwritten code of the Bel. You have attacked another human being with the idea, not to restrain or merely subdue him, but of killing him. This is the one line that we cannot, as a rule, cross.

"On the other hand," he said, coming to rest his hand on Jonny's shoulder, "we gave you invaders no instructions for a reason. We wanted you to make your own moral decisions, to decide the rightness and wrongness of your acts without the constraint of authoritarian advice. In the light of the cause which possesses your being, the rectification, in any way, of the evil done to your planet Eliyahu, what you did was at least understandable. Indeed, in the light of your nature, necessary and just."

"I only regret," Jonny said, meeting Baqa's gaze squarely, "that it was but an image that I shot."

"Let me finish," Baqa said.

"Aye," Jonny said softly.

"But events have dealt with the Emperor in their own way," Baqa continued, "and this kind of fate has no recourse. We would have tried him, we the Bel. It would not have been for us to stoop to his level. And the trial would have been a fair one, make no mistake. There would have been a defense, and the jury would have been chosen from the truly indifferent, the apathetic. But as it stands, of course, he has lost it all and can do nothing to recover it.

"But Paul and Shimmy here saw your face when you aimed at the obelisk, and they saw not anger there, not revenge. They saw calmness. Peace. Certainty. There was a rightness within you, formed out of experience by the light within. That we do not agree with the action that was the result is not relevant. You are a true k'ratika, and have learned to act not through anger, but through the rightness in your soul.

"So we will not condemn you. Rather, we will try to convince you that what we would have done, as opposed to what you tried to do, is right.

"And you may continue to live among us."

There was a long silence in the room. Jonny's face showed no emotion. Perhaps there was relief there. Probably not. Probably he had been prepared to accept anything, and was also prepared to accept this.

Shimmy broke the mood.

"You poor sap," he said with exaggerated pity. "That means you'll have to listen to us preach at you for the rest of your life!"

"A fate worse than death, to be sure," Ludwig said

heartily. And once again, laughter lived in Paul's sickroom. Paul strained mightily to hold it down. His ribs would not be able to take it.

Shimmy spoke again. "Now I have a question," he said. "Baqa, what do you mean, 'if we stay in their company'?" Paul's interest quickened. "'If we stay in their company,'" Shimmy quoted. "You imply some other choice. What is it?"

Baqa and Sylva exchanged glances.

"We might as well tell them," she said.

"Aye," Baga said. "So we might."

Sylva took up the lead.

"Neither Baqa nor I feel like living among a people that distrusts and hates us." Baqa shook his head in such comic agreement that Paul nearly choked himself to keep from laughing.

"Rather," Sylva said, "we will go out to the stars. We like Bel companionship. We have a family here, nearly a nation. Many of us will become Explorers, a much safer occupation now than it has been, by the way, given that we have Empty screens for protection and instant transport back to our home planets. We will chart out the stars for humankind."

"Aye," Baqa said. "Of course many will stay behind, the administrators and businessmen among us. But someone has to go out in ships like the *Funakoshi* and plant the Empty that will be mankind's signpost from now on. Someone has to bring the Empire beyond the stagnant Three Hundred Suns, to Four Hundred, Five Hundred, until they are beyond counting."

"You're a natural-born preacher," Jonny growled. "But despite that, I am going with you."

"I expected you would," Ahm Baqa said, looking sidelong over his mustache at the boy who had become a man.

Paul looked into Shimmy's eyes, and saw the same thing there that he knew was in his own. Baqa, Sylva, Jonny—they would not be going alone.

And luck? What is there to say about it, in the end?

In truth, the Emperor had been deluded, to think that the lucky were any threat to him. For again, there was no guessing what direction luck would take in each human being. Paul's way had led to violence and pain, and also to a freedom that few men would ever know. To the strength of k'rati, and the calmness of moral certainty. Not to riches. Not to genius. And certainly not to power over other men.

And the end was a beginning, as it always was. The beginning of a new life, or one should say a new direction in life, a new path with an uncertain, unseen goal.

But a goal was unnecessary. It was the path that was important. It was living a life fully, and rightly, and *happily*. It was making it that way.

It was making it that way . . .

"Bel," Paul said suddenly, and every head turned toward him. "Doesn't that stand for 'belly'? I'm starving!"

Wismer, Donald
Starluck

DATE DUE	BORROWER'S NAME	
	Tammy Pickerell	
NOV 15	Troy Hopkins	
JUL 14	Nancy Scroggins	
OCT 13 1992	Dunham	
APR 14	Mirkovic	

Wismer, Donald
Starluck